DEATH AT THE ABBEY

A KIPPER COTTAGE MYSTERY

JAN DURHAM

INKUBATOR
BOOKS

Published by Inkubator Books
www.inkubatorbooks.com

Copyright © 2022 by Jan Durham

ISBN (Paperback): 978-1-915275-15-8
ISBN (eBook): 978-1-915275-14-1
ISBN (Hardback) 978-1-915275-19-6

1

It stopped raining at 6.20 am. It had been raining for four days straight – nothing new in Yorkshire – and Liz had grown used to the insistent percussion on the pantiled roof of Kipper Cottage. The sudden silence jerked her out of sleep. Only the call of a lone gull could be heard, far out to sea, until St Mary's church bell clanged the half hour, high on the clifftop above her, at 6.30 am. She sighed. There was no point trying to go back to sleep – her alarm clock was due to go off any minute.

She lay in bed, wondering why she felt so terrible first thing in the morning. Waking up was always the worst, harder even than eating her meals or watching a movie alone, or going to bed without a goodnight kiss. It had been almost five years since she'd been on her own, but every morning felt as if it was the first. She sighed again, hating her own self-pity, but also knowing that beating herself up about it would only make things worse.

Scratch, scratch, scratch. And there he was. Her alarm clock. She sat up and swung her legs out of bed.

The scratching continued, with increasing urgency, as Liz

pulled on underwear, jeans and a jumper and carefully negotiated the wooden stairs down to the kitchen/living room.
The wood on some of the stairs was so rotten she might put
her foot through them. There was only one main room on
each floor, and each floor was connected by a narrow wooden
staircase hidden in a cupboard. It was more like a treehouse
than a cottage, really, thought Liz. Or a ship. Whitby had
been built by seafaring people – fishermen, whalers and
sailors. Yes. Kipper Cottage was just like an old fishing coble
that had sailed through too many storms and was taking in
water by the bucketful.

The kitchen door was rattling alarmingly by the time she
reached it.

'For heaven's sake.' She tried to push it open, but something was stopping it. 'Get back, and let me in.' The door
eventually yielded. Nelson the English bull terrier retreated
into the middle of the room and grinned up at her. With a
black patch over one of his eyes, a massive, coffin-shaped
head and disproportionately small body, he was, without
doubt, the ugliest dog in Yorkshire. But he made her smile
every time she looked at him, even at 6.30 in the morning.

He had woken her up at that time, without fail, every
morning since he'd arrived from the RSPCA shelter five
months before. She had briefly considered letting him sleep
in the bedroom with her, wondering if it might help settle
him, but quickly dismissed the idea. It was important they
should have their own space.

'Do I have time for a cup of tea?' she asked him.

He gave a little yip and did a jig of impatience. She
sighed. 'I suppose I can have one later.' She eyed the kettle on
the ancient gas stove with regret as she pushed her feet into
her Wellington boots, took her padded coat from the hook by
the front door – just in case the rain started again – and
clipped Nelson's lead onto his collar.

Outside on Henrietta Street, the air was rain-fresh, salted with the sea and only the faintest whiff of smoke from the kipper house next door. They hadn't lit the fires yet, but in a couple of hours' time the whole street would smell like a damp sweater left outside on bonfire night.

Liz tried to close the door, but the wood had swollen from the rain. She eventually had to resort to banging it shut, hoping with a wince that she hadn't woken any of her neighbours. The reverberation caused one of the screws on the house sign to tumble out, and the whole thing to swing on the single remaining screw. Liz ignored it. It was far from the only thing in Kipper Cottage that needed fixing.

She turned left, as she always did, and headed for the abbey steps. Her spirits rose as she strode down Henrietta Street still slick with rain. With its whitewashed cottages, cobbles, and old-fashioned street lamps, it was easy to imagine she'd stepped back in time. A figure in a high-viz jacket appeared around the corner, breaking the spell. The red-cheeked fishmonger tugged his cart of fresh herrings towards her, headed for the smokehouse.

'Mornin', Mrs McLuckie!'

'Morning, Mike. Lovely morning.'

'Now that bloody rain's stopped.' Mike had a van, but knew better than to try to take it down Henrietta Street, because there was nowhere to turn around. The street ended – quite literally – in the sea. The cottages at the end of the terrace had been swept into the water by a landslide from the cliff a few years before. It was only a matter of time before Kipper Cottage went the same way, but it didn't worry Liz. She'd be long gone by then.

'Wotcha, Nelson.' Mike clicked his tongue at Nelson as he passed, but the dog didn't condescend to look at him. He was on a mission. Namely, to get up the abbey steps as fast as possible so he could be off the lead.

They soon reached the bottom of the steps. As always, Liz's soul shrank a little as she looked up at them – all one hundred and ninety-nine – that wound their way up to the ruin of the once-great Benedictine Abbey on the clifftop. They were wide and shallow, worn smooth by innumerable feet through the centuries: churchgoers, pilgrims, holiday-makers and thrill-seekers hoping for a glimpse of the spooky ruins that had inspired Bram Stoker's *Dracula*.

Liz started to climb. She always counted the steps on her way up, although it really wasn't necessary, as every tenth step was marked with a Roman numeral. She was careful to avoid the worn hollows in the steps, still puddled with rain-water. Halfway up, she paused to catch her breath on one of the wider coffin steps, so-called because they allowed pall-bearers to take a rest on their way up to the church. Eigh-teenth-century Whitby lay immediately below her – a jumble of cottages with red tiled roofs. Opposite, about half a mile away, stood the grand Edwardian buildings of the West Cliff, painted cream and pastel colours. A stretch of pewter water lay in between – the harbour – where three fishing boats were currently moored. To the right of the harbour, a stone pier pointed crookedly out to sea. There was another pier too, curving round on the east side below her, but Liz wasn't able to see it from where she stood. The view was spectacular, unchanged for centuries, apart from a rash of satellite dishes and cross-hatching of phone lines.

Nelson pulled on his lead. She took a deep breath of sea air and resumed her climb. A couple of minutes later they reached the top. In front of her, in the distance, stood the gaunt ruins of the abbey church. Immediately to her left, on a mound just a few feet away, loomed the Celtic cross of St Caedmon, and beyond that squatted the parish church of St Mary's.

Liz took the left-hand path, around the church. It skirted

the eighteenth-century churchyard, its gravestones leaning into each other like drunkards. It always gave her a little frisson of horror to think that some of the gravestones marked empty graves – memorials to occupants who had been lost at sea or in far-off lands. In spite of its spooky air, this was the place Nelson loved best, for it was home not only to corpses, but a lively warren of rabbits. He heaved on his lead, threatening to pull her over.

'Okay, okay! Hold your horses.'

He squealed with impatience until she unclipped the lead, then shot off between the gravestones like a particularly un-aerodynamic bullet. His head was so large compared to his body that Liz always marvelled he could run at all, without pitching forward onto his nose. He defied all the laws of physics. He'd never caught a rabbit since he'd been living with her, and she doubted he ever would. But he clearly lived in hope.

Liz continued her walk, between the high church walls and the cliff, where only a double stretch of wire, threaded with bindweed, separated her from the perilous drop. If she climbed over it, she knew she'd be able to look down onto Henrietta St and her two adjacent cottages – Kipper Cottage and Gull Cottage. She didn't want to, and it wasn't just because a gust of wind might tug her over the edge of the cliff, but that she didn't want to see the state of the cottages' roofs. Some things were better not to know.

She'd bought them only a couple of months before, with the intention of living in one and renting out the other as a holiday let. But first there was a *lot* of work to do. She'd decided to live in the marginally less knackered one – Kipper Cottage – while she renovated Gull Cottage next door. Which certainly made sense, but what she hadn't bargained for was her own lack of stamina when it came to having to live with the ugly cladding in Kipper Cottage every day. To paraphrase

Oscar Wilde, either it would have to go, or she would. But first, she had to take out the gas fire. If she didn't, she could knock one of the gas pipes when she removed the cladding, and potentially cause a leak. The fire was a 1970s monstrosity she wanted rid of anyway, and Ryan the gas fitter was coming the next day to disconnect it. When he'd gone, she could maybe take a crowbar to the walls? She hoped the cladding was hiding original eighteenth-century panelling, or even an inglenook fireplace. Or maybe she should start by ripping up some of the carpet? She really couldn't make up her mind.

A distant yip interrupted her thoughts. It came from somewhere off to her right, in the heart of the churchyard. She paused for a moment, listening, then hurried in the direction it had come from. Maybe she was wrong? Maybe today *was* Nelson's lucky day? Lucky for him, but not so lucky for some poor old rabbit. She broke into a run, girding herself for an intervention.

When she turned the corner of the church, she saw Nelson about twenty metres away, standing over something that lay between the headstones. She thought at first it was a pile of old clothes, but as she ran towards him over the soggy, uneven ground, she quickly revised her opinion.

'Nelson! Come here!'

He ignored her, continuing to prod the prone man with his nose. He nuzzled his cheek, trying to revive him. Liz stifled a curse and ran to catch hold of the dog.

'Stay still, for heaven's sake.' As she bent to clip Nelson on his lead, he jumped up and licked her full on the lips. 'Ewwww!' She wiped her mouth with her sleeve, grabbed the bouncing dog by the scruff of his neck and finally managed to clip him on the lead.

'Come away.'

She hauled Nelson further off and stared at the man on the ground. She knew a dead body when she saw one.

2

'And what time was that, do you reckon?'

'A couple of minutes to seven. The church struck the hour while I was making the call.'

The young police officer scribbled something in his note-book, then peered back at Liz. He had a long, lugubrious face, more suited to a Victorian undertaker than a policeman. 'If you don't mind me saying so, Mrs McLuckie, you're very calm.'

'I used to be a nurse. An accident and emergency nurse.'

'Ah.' He nodded. That made sense. 'You didn't see anyone else up here at all?'

'Not a soul.'

They were sitting in the Visitor Centre car park, which had been closed and now held half a dozen squad cars and an ambulance. The ambulance had arrived with its lights flashing, but had long since switched them off. Liz was perched comfortably in the front seat of one of the squad cars, with her legs out the door, sipping a cup of coffee someone had produced from a flask. Two officers were with her, the mournful-looking one asking questions, and another crouched by her feet, feeding Nelson a sandwich.

'He's a sweetheart, isn't he?'

'When he wants to be.' Liz eyed her dog, who decided at that moment to abandon every shred of dignity and roll over onto his back, exposing his pink stomach. 'When there's food involved.'

At the sound of raised voices, Liz looked up. A middle-aged woman in a red Mini Clubman was arguing with one of the policemen guarding the main entrance to the car park. Liz recognised Dora Spackle, head curator of the Abbey Museum, clearly unhappy at not being able to get in and open up. Liz glanced at Nelson and was relieved to see he was still on his back. Hopefully, he wouldn't spot her. Following an altercation the year before, involving one of Dora's hand-bags and a kick that had, thankfully, missed its target, Dora had become Nelson's arch-nemesis. He tried to take a chunk out of her whenever he could. Or at least, he gave a very convincing impression of trying to take a chunk out of her. Liz didn't think he actually *would*, but preferred not to put it to the test. The red mini reversed away from the entrance at speed. Liz relaxed.

'Heads up!' The officer nudged his colleague with his foot. He and Liz followed his gaze to see two figures duck under the crime scene tape that stretched across the church gates on the far side of the car park. The dog-loving officer jumped up and scurried off as the two figures approached. The figure in front wore a beautifully cut grey skirt suit, at odds with her trainers and long-legged stride. Her hair was expertly coloured and cut into a bob. It was hard to tell how old she might be, exactly. Liz thought it could be anywhere between forty and fifty. The man hurrying to catch up with her was in his late twenties, wearing a puffer jacket over a suit, shirt and tie, with the freshly scrubbed look of an altar boy. The woman stopped a few yards from Liz and glared at her.

'Is this her?'

'Yes, ma'am.' The constable who'd been taking Liz's statement actually clicked his heels together. Liz smothered a smile and looked around. The woman could only be talking about her, so why the hell didn't she address her directly? She glanced at the young man behind the woman and thought she detected a flicker of embarrassment.

'I understand you found the body?' This time the question *was* directed at Liz.

'Yes,' she said. 'Nelson did.'

The female detective glared down at the dog, who, sensing hostility, sat up.

'How close did he get?'

'He, um ... pretty close, I'm afraid.'

'Please tell me he didn't touch it.'

Liz grimaced.

'Couldn't you tell it was a crime scene?'

'He was off the lead. I couldn't even see him at the time.'

'For f—' The woman rolled her eyes and addressed the young man behind her. 'Why can't people control their animals?'

'I'm sorry.' Liz stood up. 'We haven't been introduced.'

The woman seemed surprised. 'I'm Detective Inspector Flint, North Yorkshire Serious Crime Unit, and this is Detective Constable Ossett.'

'You think it could be murder, then?' asked Liz.

Flint ignored her. She glared instead at the uniformed officer. 'Have you taken her statement yet?'

'Not as yet, ma'am. We were just attempting to ascertain precisely when the body was discovered.' Liz noted his newly formal language. It wasn't lost on the young detective either, who stifled a grin.

'That's not a priority, Williams,' snapped Flint. 'The body's probably been here all night. When you've finished—'

'Excuse me,' interrupted Liz. 'But I don't think it has.'

'What?'

'It hasn't been here all night.'

DI Flint raised an eyebrow. Her weapon of choice. Liz wasn't cowed.

'I'd say it'd been here an hour at most.'

DI Flint directed a faux-amused glance at the two men. 'This one thinks she's Miss Marple.'

'I'm not that old. Not much older than you, I'm guessing.'

Flint's face blanked. The young detective looked from Liz to Flint and opened his mouth to speak. Liz cut in again.

'Humour me?'

'Okay.' Flint crossed her arms and addressed the two men. 'Let's humour her.' To Liz: 'What makes you think it wasn't there overnight?'

'It stopped raining at 6.20.'

'So? The body was wet.'

'Not with rainwater.'

Flint stared hard at Liz. 'What?'

'It's wet with brine. With seawater.'

'I know what brine is. How do you know that?'

'Nelson licked the man's face and then licked me. It was salty. Plus, if you look closely, you can see white residue on his clothes where they're beginning to dry. If he'd been in the rain for any length of time, the brine would have been diluted. It was raining all night until 6.20. I'd say the man – whoever he is – was in the graveyard an hour at most.'

No one said anything.

Flint's mouth, which had been hanging ever-so-slightly open during Liz's monologue, snapped into a line. She turned on her heel and strode off. The young detective hurried after her.

'Tell the forensic team there'll be dog saliva on the body. And hairs too, probably. For the love of God, Ossett, save me from people who watch too much bloody TV. Save me from everyone who thinks they can do our job.'

Her voice carried back to where Liz stood. The constable cleared his throat.

'Sorry,' he said. 'The new DI can be a bit ...' He hesitated, grasping for words.

'Rude?'

'I was going to say a bit of a nightmare. But please don't tell her I said that.'

BY THE TIME Liz had given a full statement at the police station, it was gone eleven o'clock.

'Are you sure you don't want a lift home?' Constable Williams asked her, his long face breaking into a smile. 'It's no bother.'

'We're fine, thanks. A leg stretch will do us good.' Nowhere in the town was more than forty minutes' walk away. 'And I know you'll be keen to get back up to the abbey.'

The constable's expression became glum again. Liz suspected he would rather keep out of DI Flint's way.

As she stepped out with Nelson onto the pavement in front of the unlovely seventies-style police station, her stomach rumbled, and she realised with some surprise, she'd eaten nothing all day. Nelson looked up at her accusingly.

'What's *your* problem?' she asked him. 'You've had at least two ham sandwiches.'

He didn't deny it. They set off to walk home through the town. As they got closer to the main shopping area, the streets grew busier with holidaymakers flushed from their bed and breakfast accommodation by the sunshine. The sun was warm on Liz's face as she walked, and, in spite of the disturbing events of the morning, she felt well-being wash through her. She'd never regretted coming to Whitby. It was a place that held nothing but happy memories, of sandy days on the beach, eating fish and chips, and exploring cobbled yards and alleys with her sister, Julie. They used to come every year for their summer holidays, making the long drive down from Edinburgh in their dad's battered work van, bumping across the North York moors, competing with each other to see who would be the first to spot the sea.

As Liz and Nelson reached the harbour, she saw the swing bridge was open. It was the only route over to the old town, so they had to wait with the tourists as a yacht passed slowly through, on its way to the marina. The bridge inched closed, the barriers went up, and a bell rang to say it was safe to cross. Everyone who'd been waiting sprinted off across the bridge like racehorses out of a starting gate. Liz wondered why everyone was in such a hurry. Weren't they supposed to be on holiday? She set a more leisurely pace, enjoying the view of harbour as she crossed. Once over the bridge, she turned left into Sandgate, the narrow, cobbled heart of the old town, lined with small shops selling souvenirs, books, ice cream and handmade jewellery. She thought about popping into the Full Moon Café for a toastie and a chat, but changed her mind when she got there. Through the Dickensian bow windows she could see it was heaving with customers. She spotted Tilly's bright bandana bobbing about as she waited on tables, and, not wanting to add to her friend's workload, Liz kept walking. She'd have something at home. She was pretty sure she had some sausages in the fridge and some rolls that weren't too far past their best. She kept going past the Old Town Hall into Church Street, similar to Sandgate but slightly broader, and busier. The thought of Kipper Cottage was suddenly very alluring. Nelson must have sensed it too, for he speeded up.

The abbey steps were a lot busier than they'd been when she'd climbed them earlier, but the crowd thinned almost completely once they'd passed them. It was with a sense of relief that Liz eyed her newly wonky house sign, put her key in the door of Kipper Cottage, and stepped inside.

She closed the door, cutting off the distant sounds of the town. In the sudden calm, other thoughts rushed in, ones she'd been pushing to the back of her mind ever since she left the police station.

What was the dead man doing on the clifftop? Who was he? And how did he die?

3

'What was he doing up there? How did he die?'

'I have no idea. There were no marks on him that I could see, but he was lying face down.'

'Odd.' Benedict held out his hand without looking at her. 'Pass the pepper grinder, would you?'

She hurried to do as he asked, and watched as he ground black pepper expertly onto the plates of bruschetta in front of him. She saw he had a large sticking plaster on one of his index fingers.

'A slip of the knife while I was chopping tomatoes.' He grinned at her. 'Just as well tomatoes are red.'

'Lovely.' She was pretty sure he was joking.

They were in the kitchen of his house at Pannet Park, rightly known by locals as the 'posh' part of town. It was a big Edwardian house, set back from the road, screened by a beech hedge, with glorious views of the park and its glasshouses. The kitchen was large but welcoming, with chunky cabinets, a butler's sink, and the Aga always on, even in summer.

'There.' He sprinkled chives on the slices and stepped back to admire his handiwork. He ran a hand through his hair. The flashes of white in it were the only thing that betrayed his fifty-something years; otherwise he was lean and athletic, almost boyish looking. Liz put it down to his love of cycling and the twinkle of intelligence in his eyes. She had always found that twinkle especially attractive in a man. Not that she was attracted to Benedict. He was just a friend.

'Bring this through, will you?' He gave her one of the plates.

She followed him through into the conservatory. It wasn't a modern lean-to, but something truly worthy of the name, with soaring panes of glass, tropical plants and wicker furniture. They put the plates on the dresser. The table was set up for mah-jong, the tile wall already built and the tile racks in their usual places, waiting for the players.

'Just chuck Delilah off there.' Benedict pointed to one of the chairs and its occupant. 'She'll soon find somewhere else to drape herself.' Delilah was one of half a dozen elderly cats that shared Benedict's house, a legacy from his late wife, Katherine. Katherine had died six months before, but Liz had never known her. She and Benedict had met since, through the local Historical Society, and immediately hit it off, even before they discovered a mutual love of mah-jong. They met up with two other players – Benedict's son, Kevin, and Liz's friend Tilly – every Thursday night to play.

Benedict settled his long limbs on the cane sofa.

'So where was he, exactly?' he asked.

'About forty feet from the north wall of the church.'

'Not really on the way to anywhere.'

'No.'

'Could it have been an accident?'

'I thought it must have been at first. Or a heart attack or something. But *someone* called Serious Crimes.'

'A mystery,' said Benedict. 'I daresay we'll find out soon enough.'

Liz looked at her watch. It wasn't like Kevin to be late. Tilly, of course, was a different matter: Liz had never known her to be on time for anything.

'He's been having trouble at work.' Benedict had either seen her look at her watch, or read her mind. 'A new boss, apparently. I've told him it's just one of those things you have to deal with. But you know Kevin.'

'Too nice for his own good.'

The doorbell rang, and Benedict got up to answer it. There was a flurry of activity in the hall, and Tilly heralded her arrival with a jingle of bells and a waft of patchouli oil before pouncing into the room, wearing a long Indian print skirt and a neon green T-shirt. They didn't really go together, or with her cropped peroxide hair. She should have looked like a bag lady, but just looked achingly cool.

'Christ, B, it's boiling in here. Why do you always have the heating on?' She wrestled her cardigan off, revealing the tattoo on her forearm, a busty '50s pin-up girl with the motto *Not your darling.*

'Hiya, gorgeous.' She kissed Liz on the cheek. 'Did I see you sneak past the café at lunchtime?'

'I was going to come in, but thought I'd show mercy.'

Tilly groaned. 'We were bonkers busy. I suppose it was because the rain had stopped. Everyone comes out with the sun.'

That was true, especially in Whitby, where holidaymakers were always desperate to get out of their B&Bs and onto the beach.

'Ohhhh ... these look nice.' Tilly had spotted the bruschetta. 'Can I have one?'

'Be my guest,' said Benedict. 'I have no idea where Kevin's got to.'

They all helped themselves to food and settled down to eat. Tilly took a cat off her chair and put it on her knee. She seemed oblivious to its claws as it kneaded her through the thin material of her skirt.

'Oh! Did you hear?' she said around a mouthful of tomato. 'They found a body this morning on the East Cliff!'

Benedict glanced at Liz.

'Everyone's saying it's a suicide.'

'I don't think so,' said Liz.

'What makes you say that?'

'I found him.'

Tilly's eyes saucered. 'No!'

'If he killed himself,' said Liz, 'it wasn't obvious.'

'I wonder where Kevin is,' said Benedict, forestalling further questions from Tilly.

Liz licked a crumb off her finger. 'Perhaps his crabby new boss is making him work overtime.'

Just then, as if conjured by the words, they heard a key in the front door.

'Sorry I'm late!' Kevin called out from the hall.

'Come in and get something to eat,' called Benedict.

A moment later, Kevin – otherwise known as DC Ossett – wandered into the conservatory. Benedict nodded at his shirt and tie.

'Have you come straight from work?' he asked.

Kevin nodded. 'It's been a hell of a day.' He caught Liz's eye. 'I imagine Liz has told you all about it.'

'No, she hasn't,' said Tilly. 'I've just got here. Come on, spill the beans. Give us the details, the gorier the better.'

'Not much to tell, really. It's all a bit of a mystery.' He turned to Liz. 'I'm so sorry about Flint. I did try to tell her I know you, but she didn't listen.' His schoolboy features crumpled with dismay. 'She never listens.'

'Don't worry about it.' Liz stood up and went to the

dresser. She put a slice of bruschetta on a plate, poured a glass of wine, and took them to Kevin.

'I do worry about it,' he said with a look of despair. 'I don't know how long I'm going to last, to be honest. She finds fault with everything I do.'

'From what I could see,' said Liz, 'she does that with everyone.'

'True,' agreed Kevin, 'but no one else has to work with her one-on-one. It's like carrying a hand grenade in your pocket. She can go off at any time, literally, about anything. Yesterday she went on a ten-minute rant – ten whole minutes – because someone hadn't filled some machine or other in the ladies' toilet.'

'To be fair,' said Liz, 'I'd probably go on a rant about that, too. There's nothing worse than being caught short when you need ...' She saw Kevin blush, and thought, not for the first time, that his choice of career really was astonishing. She changed the subject. 'Did I detect a Middlesbrough accent?'

Kevin nodded. 'She transferred six weeks ago. It was a promotion, but I think they were glad to get rid of her.'

Tilly had been watching the exchange with an expression of growing disbelief.

'For the love of God!' she burst out. 'I can't believe you two are chattering on about office politics and Tampax when there's stuff we really should be talking about.'

Everyone looked at her.

'The dead body?' She turned to Kevin. 'Who was he? You must be able to give us a name, at least?'

Kevin nodded, but couldn't speak until he'd swallowed his food. 'We found a driver's license in his pocket. Ian Crowby.'

'Professor Crowby?' Benedict paused with his glass halfway to his mouth.

'You know him?' asked Kevin.

'Not really,' said Benedict. 'I've met him a few times, through work.'

Kevin nodded. 'I thought you might. He's chief curator for YMD.'

'YMD?' prompted Tilly.

'Yorkshire Museum Development. They help museums sort out their collections, to display and conserve them.'

'Not a dangerous profession, then,' said Tilly, disappointed.

'Unless you're particularly clumsy.' Benedict laughed at his own joke.

'When did you find him, Liz?' asked Tilly.

Liz was staring at Benedict.

'Liz?'

She snapped her attention back.

'Sorry. Um ... yes. It was when I was taking Nelson for a walk.'

'And he was dead?'

'Very.'

There was a pause.

'Dear God, it's like trying to get blood from a stone!' Tilly rolled her eyes. 'Dead HOW? Dead WHERE? Dead WHEN? Will somebody please answer some bloody questions?'

'Well, pardon me for not satisfying your morbid curiosity,' said Kevin. 'We don't know much yet ... he has bruises on his face and neck, but the early signs are that he drowned.'

'Drowned?' echoed Tilly. 'On the clifftop?'

Benedict's eyebrows rose.

'Someone must have carried him up there afterwards,' said Liz.

'Or drove him to the car park,' said Kevin.

'Why would they do that?' Liz frowned. 'There was no attempt to hide the body, as far as I could see.'

'That's true,' said Kevin.

'Perhaps it was a statement,' said Liz.

'What do you mean?' asked Kevin.

'I don't know … a warning of some kind, to someone?'

'Also,' said Kevin, 'he had a fish in his pocket.'

They all stared at him.

'What kind of fish?' asked Benedict.

Kevin shrugged. 'I don't know. Quite a small one.'

'It must have swum in there,' said Tilly, 'while he was drowning.'

They pondered that for a while. Liz thought it was unlikely.

'You know,' said Tilly, 'I once watched an episode of something or other where they found a waterskier in the desert. It turned out he'd been scooped up accidentally from the sea by one of those firefighting planes and dropped onto a fire.'

'Ingenious,' said Liz. 'The things these writers come up with.'

'Ingenious,' agreed Benedict, 'but not very likely.'

Tilly looked at Kevin hopefully.

'We don't have planes like that in Yorkshire, Tills. And even if we did, there was no fire.'

'Plus, he was fully dressed,' said Liz.

'Oh.' Tilly didn't look too disappointed. She took another bite of tomato and spoke around it. 'It was just a thought.'

'There has to be an explanation.' Liz finished her bruschetta and dusted crumbs off her jeans. 'It must make sense to someone.'

'I suppose it must,' agreed Kevin. 'But the question is, who?'

'That isn't the really important question,' said Benedict.

'Oh?' Kevin looked at him.

'The important question is … does anyone want to play

mah-jong tonight? Or have I fed you all this delicious food for nothing?'

WHEN THEY TOOK a break at nine o'clock, Liz managed to corner Benedict alone in the kitchen.

'You knew Ian Crowby quite well, didn't you?'

'What makes you think that?' He didn't look at her, but busied himself refilling glasses.

'Because you were so keen to change the subject. And your jokes. A bit inappropriate under the circumstances. Plus —' she hesitated, wondering whether to let him in on her secret '—you have a tell.'

'A tell?' *Now* he looked at her.

'Mm.' Liz nodded and took a sip of wine. 'The left-hand corner of your mouth twitches when you lie. It twitched about half an hour ago when you told Tilly you weren't collecting white dragons. Five minutes later, you put down a pong of them. And it twitched when you said you didn't really know Ian Crowby.'

'I spent a few days with him last year, when he helped us with our Knots display.' Benedict was an expert on maritime antiques and volunteered at the Captain Cook Memorial Museum in Grape Lane a few times a week. 'I suppose I didn't admit it because I was shocked.'

'What was he like?'

'A pain in the arse.' He saw she was watching his mouth. 'Am I telling the truth?'

'Yes.' She smiled. 'Ian Crowby was definitely a pain in the arse. Or at least *you* think so. In what way?'

'Oh, I don't know. He was one of those men who talked about women as if they were a different species. We had a lot of them in the Navy, usually from single-sex public schools. And he was horribly pompous. Loved the sound of his own

voice, but knew nothing, really, about maritime history. Also
—' Benedict paused dramatically '—he couldn't tell a double
bowline from a cleat hitch!'

'Good God.'

'Exactly.' Benedict grinned. 'I am sorry he's dead, though.
Obviously.'

'Obviously.' It took all of Liz's self-control not to look at
his mouth.

4

The faux-wood cladding was the tackiest Liz had ever seen, and was stuck to the walls of the kitchen/living room with thick glue turned yellow with age. When it came off the walls, it would probably take most of the plaster with it, another costly job she hadn't anticipated when she'd bought the cottages.

There was no fireplace, just a wall of blank panelling behind it, but when she'd lifted a corner of the hideous swirly carpet, she'd spotted stone beneath. Possibly a hearth. Many of the cottages in the old town had big inglenook fireplaces, completely out of proportion for the size of the rooms and not very practical in terms of heat retention, but atmospheric and very beautiful. With a lot of good luck, the cladding could be hiding an inglenook.

But first, the fire.

She sipped her tea and checked her watch, ignoring Nelson's baleful glare from the other side of the room. She hadn't taken him up the steps to the abbey that morning. No doubt the police were still there, and she really couldn't face the drama so early. So instead she had walked Nelson along

Church Street and cut down one of the narrow alleyways known locally as 'ghauts' onto the rocky shore. A long enough walk for Nelson to do the necessary, but woefully lacking in rabbits. Now, Nelson stared at her accusingly from his basket.

'Oh, for heaven's sake, get over it,' she said. 'I'll take you out again later.'

He huffed and lay down, turning his back on her, but was up again almost immediately, as someone knocked on the door. He leapt towards it with a yip.

'Get down!' She grabbed the dog with one hand and opened the door with the other. 'Come in, Ryan. Don't worry about him. He doesn't bite.'

'It's okay, Mrs McLuckie.' The gas fitter dumped his tools on the floor and greeted the dog, ruffling his head and ears. 'I'm used to dogs. Hello. You're a fine lad, aren't you?' Nelson surrendered to Ryan's praise, licking his big callused and scarred hands.

'Would you like a cup of tea before you start?'

'I won't, if you don't mind. I have another couple of jobs to fit in before I take the afternoon off.'

Then Liz remembered. 'I was sorry to hear about your mum.'

Ryan's blunt, good-natured features softened.

'Aye, well, it was a long time coming. It's a terrible thing to say, but if I'm honest, it was something of a relief.'

Liz knew what he meant. His mum had died of cancer, and it had taken her the same way it had taken Mark, piece by piece. It was five years now since Mark had died, but Liz could remember that night in the hospice when he had slipped away as if it was yesterday. She'd felt grief, certainly – a hollow, howling loss – but also release. And then guilt for feeling relieved. Bereavement was a complicated business.

'What time is the funeral?'

'Two thirty. Up at St Mary's. You're very welcome.'

'Thank you.' She hadn't really known Ryan's mother to speak to, and would probably feel like an interloper. But she might go anyway.

Ryan nodded. 'Right. Where's your gas meter?'

Yorkshiremen weren't known for displays of emotion.

IT TOOK him less than half an hour to disconnect the gas fire and lift it out.

'It's a bit of a beast,' he said. 'Do you want me to get rid of it for you?'

'Can you?'

'No problem. I'll back the van up. But first, I'll reconnect the gas.'

As he came back from the meter cupboard, he spotted the gas stove.

'Have you had that checked?'

'No. Do you think I should?'

He eyed her with a hint of amusement. 'It must be at least forty years old. By rights, I shouldn't let you use it.'

Her dismay showed on her face.

He grinned. 'I can come back tomorrow and give it the once-over?'

'You're a star.'

'If it's not okay, I'll have to disconnect it, though.'

She nodded. Better safe than sorry. That was the problem with renovating old houses. You start off trying to do one thing, but then discover that something else needs doing first, but you can't do *that* until you've fixed something else ... and suddenly you're stuck in a vortex, draining time and money.

Ryan grunted as he lifted the fire. She hurried to open the door, and he manhandled it out.

'See you tomorrow,' he said.

· · ·

WHEN HE'D GONE, Liz sighed and dropped into her armchair. She really wanted another cup of tea, but didn't feel she could use the stove before Ryan had checked it. Also, if she was honest, she felt quite low. She didn't know whether it was her discovery of Ian Crowby's body the day before, or talking to Ryan about his mum, but the dark days of Mark's illness and death had come rushing back. Time doesn't so much heal grief as harden it, like ice forming on a lake. It stays thin in places, and you can tumble through at any time.

She gave herself a shake. 'Get a grip, woman.'

She looked at the space where the fire used to be, got up and tapped the cladding. Hollow. There was definitely a void there. She spotted a join in the sheets near where the fire had been, and managed to wriggle the tip of her finger into it. She heaved. Then heaved again. CRACK. A triangular piece of cladding about the size of a dinner plate gave way to reveal a black hole. Liz knelt beside it and peered in. It seemed to be filled with rubble, which didn't sound very promising, but was, in fact, exactly what she'd been hoping for. She went to fetch her crowbar, work gloves and goggles. There was nothing like physical exertion for taking your mind off things.

TWO HOURS LATER, covered in dust and soot, she was staring at a jagged hole in the panelling several feet wide. And – joy of joys! – an inglenook fireplace. It was still half filled with rubble, chunks of mortar and bricks, but it had a stone lintel and what looked like the original hearth. She spotted some-thing poking out of the debris at the back. She thought at first it was a piece of pottery, but when she reached in and pulled it out, she saw it was a stone bottle, cream and brown, decorated with a sailing ship and lettering – Whitchurch & Butler, Whitby.

'GINGER BEER BOTTLES,' said Benedict. 'But that's all I can tell you. They're not really my thing.'

There had been two bottles in the rubble. The larger one with the picture of the sailing ship, and a smaller one just with lettering – P. Bagby and Sons, Whitby. Miraculously, both were intact, without a scratch or a chip on them.

'Have you had a shock or something?' asked Benedict.

'What?'

'You seem to have gone white overnight.'

'Oh. It's dust. I couldn't have a shower. No hot water.'

'You've also got rings round your eyes. Like a panda.'

Liz shrugged. 'I like pandas.'

'Me too.'

Liz swallowed. 'I had the gas disconnected for a while this morning. It's done something weird to the boiler. Luckily, Ryan's coming back tomorrow.'

'Ryan Goddard?

Liz nodded.

'I'm surprised he's working today.'

'He says it helps to keep busy.'

Benedict looked suddenly bleak. Liz hurried to distract him. 'Are you going to the funeral?'

Benedict shook his head. 'Got to hold the fort. There's only me here this afternoon.'

They were sitting in the tiny office of the Captain Cook Memorial Museum in Grape Lane, a narrow building four storeys high, criss-crossed with wooden beams and filled with seafaring exhibits.

'What about you?' prompted Benedict. 'Are you going?'

'Probably not. I didn't really know Jessy Goddard, and I'm a mess.'

'You can use my shower if you like. I'll give you the keys.'

'No, it's okay. I won't be missed.' She didn't want to admit she was uncomfortable at the thought of being alone in his house.

'The police were here this morning ... not Kevin. His boss.'

'Ah. The charming Detective Inspector Flint.'

'Actually, I thought she was okay. Quite nice, in fact.'

Liz hid her surprise. She supposed old Flintface might well be on her best behaviour with an upstanding citizen like Benedict. An upstanding, *attractive* citizen like Benedict.

'She was asking about Ian's business connections in the town. I couldn't tell her much, other than that he'd spent some time here last year, and a few weeks up at the Abbey Museum with Dora Spackle.'

'I don't suppose she was able to confirm he drowned?'

Benedict shook his head. 'I suppose that's the sort of thing they prefer to keep to themselves.'

'More likely, they haven't had the post-mortem report yet.'

'More likely. Why are you so interested, anyway?'

A good question. Liz thought about it. 'I'm not sure. I suppose, having found his body, I just feel ... responsible, somehow. Does that sound weird?'

'A bit.' Benedict grinned. 'But that's one of the things I like about you.'

Blood rushed to Liz's cheeks. Luckily, Benedict was looking at the bottles on the table. 'You should take your finds to Wally Duguid. He'll probably be able to tell you more. He owns Chapel Antiques on Baxtergate.'

'I'll do that. Thanks.' Liz gathered up her bottles and fled.

. . .

AFTER WASHING her face in the ladies' loo at the museum, Liz stepped out into Grape Lane, a narrow thoroughfare thronged with tourists. She had intended to go straight to Baxtergate, but was distracted by the rumble in her stomach. Once again, she'd forgotten to eat. She made her way to Sandgate instead. Luckily, the Full Moon Café wasn't busy – it was too late for breakfast and too early for lunch – so she was able to slip into her usual table by the window. Only two of the other tables were occupied, one by a couple of well-dressed ladies, and the other by a couple trying to harangue their two toddlers into eating something. The plastic buckets and spades beside them on the floor said they were en route to the beach.

She looked around the tea room, marvelling as she usually did at the transformation Tilly and her wife, Mags, had made since they'd moved in. It used to be a chip shop, with stainless steel fittings caked with cooking fat and grease stains on the ceiling, but now it was nothing short of magical. At a raised area at one end, there was a bookshop specialising in New Age subjects – spiritualism, Tarot cards and self-help. It was an old-fashioned kind of bookshop with tall shelves and a spiral staircase up to a reading nook with a couple of battered leather chairs. The other end of the room was a tea room set up with eight or nine tables, a big pine counter showcasing home-made cakes, and a doorway with a beaded curtain leading to the kitchen. It was all decorated in the same eclectic style in which Tilly herself dressed, with battered antiques, chintzy cushions and the odd bit of retro '70s kitsch and neon thrown in. Melamine tables mixed with wooden ones, lava lamps with old-fashioned fringed standing lamps, and a sprinkling of crystals, incense burners and fairy lights were the frosting on the cake. In theory, it shouldn't have worked, but it did. Customers just seemed to relax as soon as they stepped through the door.

'Liz!' Tilly hurtled from the counter to kiss her on the cheek. 'I see you've recovered from last night.' Tilly had thrashed them all at mah-jong. She often did, but the night before, she'd been on particularly sparkling form and had shown no mercy.

'I was distracted,' said Liz with a grin. 'Finding dead bodies is very distracting.'

'Pathetic excuse.'

'What is?' Mags emerged from the beaded curtain, wiping her hands on a tea towel. She was yin to Tilly's yang, well built, with short dark hair and a hesitant smile, wearing an apron with a picture of the *Coronation Street* character Hilda Ogden, complete with curlers and dangling cigarette. A nod to Yorkshire's TV past, entirely wasted on most customers.

'Finding dead bodies,' said Tilly. 'Liz seems to think it's a good reason for her pitiful mah-jong moves last night.'

'Are you okay?' Mag's eyes were warm with concern. 'Tills told me all about it. It must have been awful.'

'It wasn't too bad. I've seen worse in A&E.' Strictly speaking, in her years as an emergency room nurse, she certainly *had* seen worse, but coming across a corpse as a 'civilian' had somehow been so much more shocking. It wasn't something she wanted to dwell on.

'Your toastie's in,' said Mags. 'It won't be a minute. You want your usual tea?'

'Please.'

Mags and Tilly disappeared through the curtain.

Liz smiled. They were the perfect couple. She had to admit she'd been a bit shocked when Tilly had told her where they'd met – in a young offender institution. Tilly had been in there for breaking and entering, and Mags for some undisclosed offence. Liz hadn't asked. She was just happy they'd found each other. Not long after they were released, Mags's aunt had died, leaving her a considerable inheritance.

After a few years travelling the world together, they'd settled in Whitby and bought the café. They seemed to be blissfully happy and firmly on the straight and narrow. To Liz, it was further proof that money – or the lack of it – was often the root of crime.

Her thoughts were disturbed by the jangle of the bell on the door. It was Iris Gladwell hauling a huge bin bag. Liz pulled out the chair beside her, indicating that Iris should join her. The old lady huffed over to her, dropped her burden and plunked onto the chair.

'TILLY!' she bellowed at the beaded curtain. 'CUP OF TEA AND A SCONE WHEN YOU'RE READY, LOVE!'

She ignored the startled glances of the two well-heeled ladies. The young couple didn't even flinch. Liz supposed that having two toddlers had made them immune to noise.

'Is that you finished for the day?' she asked Iris.

'THANK GOD.' The old lady nodded at the bin bag at her feet. 'I JUST HAVE TO DROP THIS AT THE LAUNDRY ON MY WAY HOME.' Iris was incapable of speaking at any volume less than a bellow. When Liz had first met her, she'd thought it was because she was hard of hearing, but later learned she'd always shouted like that. As a changeover cleaner for many of the Airbnbs in the town, Iris was never short of work.

'Morning, Iris.' Tilly hurried out to put Liz's teapot and toastie on the table. 'Do you want jam with your scone this morning?'

'JUST BUTTER, LOVE, TA.'

Tilly nodded and headed back to the kitchen.

'THE SEEDS GET STUCK IN MY DENTURES,' said Iris to Liz by way of explanation. 'SOMETIMES IT'S WORTH IT. I DO LOVE A BIT OF JAM. BUT I CAN'T BE ON WITH IT THIS MORNING.'

Liz wondered, not for the first time, how old Iris might be.

From her clothes and the lines on her face, Liz guessed late seventies, although the woman marched everywhere with the determination of a regimental sergeant major. She also had a voice to match.

'SOUNDS LIKE YOU HAD AN INTERESTING TIME YESTERDAY.'

'Sorry?' said Liz.

'UP AT THE ABBEY. THE REV TOLD ME YOU FOUND THE BODY.'

'Yes.' It always astonished Liz how fast news spread in the town.

'BAD BUSINESS. I WAS UP THERE FIRST THING, AT ST MARY'S, GETTING IT READY FOR THE FUNERAL. TOOK ME LONGER THAN EXPECTED, WHAT WITH ALL THE MESS.'

'Mess?'

'SOME KIDS HAD BROKEN A WINDOW IN THE STOREROOM. LEFT GLASS ALL OVER THE FLOOR.'

'When did they do that?'

'WELL, THE REV ONLY FOUND IT YESTERDAY, BUT IT PROBABLY HAPPENED THE NIGHT BEFORE.'

'The same night as the murder?'

'MURDER?' Iris's eyes grew round. 'IT WAS MURDER, THEN?'

The young couple turned to stare at her with a look of panic, then tried to distract their kids with food. Liz wanted to tell Iris to keep her voice down, but guessed she probably had no idea how loud she was.

'Did the Reverend tell the police about the break-in?' she asked instead.

Iris shook her head. 'IT WAS JUST KIDS. HAPPENS A LOT. LAST YEAR THEY TRASHED THE HARVEST FESTIVAL DISPLAY. CHUCKED VEGGIES ALL OVER THE PLACE. TOOK ME WEEKS TO GET THE CARROT STAINS

OUT OF THE FLAGSTONES. WEEKS! THE REV SAYS IT'S JUST HIGH SPIRITS, BUT I WISH I COULD GET MY HANDS ON THE LITTLE BUGGERS. I'D GIVE THEM HIGH SPIRITS!'

Liz didn't doubt it.

She thought it was odd, all the same, that there'd been a break-in at the church the same night a body had appeared in the graveyard. It didn't sound like a coincidence.

5

The funeral was well attended, with several dozen mourners. Liz didn't know how old Jessy Goddard had been, but most of her friends seemed to be in their seventies. Ryan was at the front of the church with his wife and two other women she guessed were his sisters. Liz also spotted Iris and a few other faces she recognised in the congregation. Liz sat at the back and tried not to scratch her head. She'd cleaned herself up as well as she could in cold water at Kipper Cottage, but her hair was beyond help. In the end, she'd had to resort to wearing a woolly hat that was hot and made her head itch. Not that it was warm in the church. Like most churches, it was freezing whatever the weather. From the outside, St Mary's was a typical twelfth-century building – solid and squat and not in the least decorative. Inside, however, was another matter. It had been refitted in the eighteen hundreds, with polished wooden box pews and white painted balconies supported by barley-twist posts.

The Reverend Gillian Garraway, an elfin-looking woman in her forties, delivered a moving service from the bottom level of the unusual three-storey pulpit. She'd obviously known Jessy Goddard well. Liz wondered whether the top pulpit, with its carved canopy and red velvet hangings, was ever used. Perhaps for Christmas or Easter services? Liz wasn't a churchgoer. She'd grown up in a Methodist family, although her parents went to church out of habit rather than devotion. She herself had ditched Sunday school as soon as she was old enough. Nowadays, she felt uncomfortable whenever she was in a church, as if a lightning bolt might flash through the congregation and smite her. Of course, she knew she was being irrational. If God existed, he'd have much more important things to do.

The service ended with a hymn as the coffin was lifted by the pall-bearers to be taken to the crematorium. There hadn't been any new burials at St Mary's for decades – the clifftop had simply run out of space. Plus, it wasn't safe. Several coffins had ended up on the beach at the end of Henrietta Street because of cliff erosion. Liz sat down again as the church gradually emptied to see Jessy on her final journey. She'd been in the church before, of course, but only as a sightseer. It was a fascinating place, a mix of original medieval gothic and Regency fantasy, with nooks and crannies and interesting memorial plaques.

Liz wandered up the nave, drawn by the beauty of the stained glass over the altar into the transept, between white barley-twist supports. A large marble font stood to one side at the top of the steps, its carvings worn smooth by the years. She couldn't resist stroking the cool and silky stone. As she did, she saw something – a spot of something brown on the rim. She leaned in for a closer look. It was only about half a centimetre in diameter, but very distinctive. She'd seen many, many spots exactly like it, on many hospital floors. Liz looked at the font ... at the *big* stone font ... and wondered. It was filled with what she assumed was holy water. She couldn't resist. She dipped her finger into the water and brought it to her lips. Salty!

'In the olden days, we used to lock the font,' said an amused voice. 'To protect the holy water from witches. Perhaps I should revive the practice?'

Liz whirled, to see Reverend Garraway at the bottom of the chancel steps. Liz's cheeks flamed.

'I was just ... um ... checking,' she said.

'Ah.' The reverend came up the steps to join her. She looked a little older close up. The fine lines around her eyes crinkled into a smile. 'And did it pass muster?'

'It's salty.'

'Blessed salt. We put it in the holy water. Not sure why, really. Tradition, I suppose. We *do* like our traditions in the Anglican church.' The Reverend smiled. 'Mrs McLuckie, isn't it?'

'Liz.' Liz offered her hand.

'Gillian. Pleased to meet you. I've seen you around with your dog. It was you who found poor Professor Crowby, wasn't it?'

'Yes. A bit of a shock.'

'I bet.'

'Iris Gladwell told me you had a break-in too?'

'More of a break *out*, really.' The reverend saw Liz's puzzled expression. 'They broke *in* to the storeroom, but then *out* of the side door. It was open when I arrived.'

'You don't think it had anything to do with Professor Crowby?'

'Shouldn't think so. It happens every now and again. Kids with nothing better to do.' She looked at her watch and gasped. 'Talking of which, I have a primary school group arriving in fifteen minutes.'

'You'd better get rid of the coffin trestle.'

'Absolutely!' The reverend grinned at Liz. 'Would you mind giving me a hand?'

Liz helped the reverend manhandle the trestles from the nave into the storeroom. It was a small, dusty space, crammed with folding tables, extra chairs and a stack of rarely used religious objects. There was only one window, a plain leaded light on the far wall. Liz could see that several of the panes were missing near the latch, and the lead had been twisted to make room for the intruder's hand. It couldn't have been easy to get in. The reverend followed Liz's gaze and frowned.

'I should get that boarded up. It'll be a while before we can get someone to fix it.'

'A specialist job, I should think.'

' 'Fraid so. We'll have to go on the waiting list. Still ... these things are sent to try us.' She led the way back out into the church. 'Thanks for your help, Liz. It was lovely meeting you.'

'And you.'

They shook hands again.

'Maybe I'll see you here again soon? At one of our services?'

Liz looked sharply at her, but saw she had a twinkle in her eye. Liz grinned. 'Maybe,' she said. They both knew she wouldn't.

ON HER WAY out of the church, Liz saw there was only one police car left in the car park. A crime scene officer, probably. She resisted the urge to go round the back of the church to look at the broken window from the outside. Why was she so interested in finding out who killed Ian Crowby? She might have found his body, but it was really none of her business.

Since Mark's death, she knew she'd been on autopilot. Even her decision to retire early and move to Whitby felt as if someone else had made it for her. In retrospect, the early retirement might not have been a good idea, because, if she was honest with herself, she missed the urgency and the action of the emergency room, the satisfaction of making a difference. She'd thought that having the two cottages to renovate might fill that gap. And it did. But only up to a point. There was still a whole level of her brain that didn't seem to be engaged at all. And it wasn't only that ...

Years before, not long after they were married, she and Mark had found out he couldn't father children, thanks to a particularly virulent dose of mumps when he was fourteen. They'd talked about adopting, but eventually decided not to. They both had busy, fulfilling careers and each other. Now that Mark was dead, Liz didn't regret that decision. Not really. She just hadn't been prepared for the realisation there was no one else in the world who really needed her. There were times when that bothered her.

But then she remembered – there *was* someone who needed her.

And she still owed him a proper walk.

BACK AT KIPPER COTTAGE, Liz took off her itchy hat before going out again. She might look a fright, but at least she could think straight without the constant irritation. She stared at her face in the mirror. She supposed it wasn't too bad. A few lines and wrinkles, but pleasant enough. Her hair was her best feature, thick and wavy, usually a dark golden colour, threaded here and there with silver, but today white all over with dust. A glimpse into the future? Liz decided she could live with it.

'Come on, Nelson.'

He ignored her.

'Walk?' The magic word. Nelson jumped up and wagged

his stumpy tail. She knew he wasn't going to be happy when he discovered they weren't going up to the abbey. They were going to the West Cliff. But first, she had to grab some sandwiches.

'You make the best sausage rolls,' said Kevin around a mouthful.

He broke some off and gave it to Nelson.

'Why does everyone feel compelled to feed my dog?' asked Liz. 'He hardly looks like he's starving.'

Kevin shook his head. 'It's his eyes. Derren Brown.' Kevin waggled his fingers like a hypnotist. 'You *will* feed me.'

They were sitting in one of the glass shelters on the West Cliff, which was very different to the older eastern part of the town. Most of the buildings on the esplanade were Edwardian, painted pastel colours, giving the West Cliff all the dignity and elegance of a wealthy spa resort. From where they sat, they couldn't see the art deco paddling pool, always popular with children, but they could see the beach some few hundred yards below them. The wide stretch of sand was still dotted here and there with families, even though the light was starting to fail. The sea was calm and glassy, and there was a definite sense of heaviness in the air. Even the seagulls were quiet.

'Rain again tonight,' said Kevin.

'Looks like it,' agreed Liz. She poured him some coffee from the flask Tilly had given her.

'You're a lifesaver.' He eyed her. 'I only have fifteen minutes before I have to get back. What was it you wanted to tell me?'

'Has the coroner's report come back yet?'

'I assume you mean for Ian Crowby? You were right. Death by drowning in seawater.'

'Are they sure?'

'Eh?'

'Are they sure it was *sea*water?'

Kevin looked thoroughly confused. 'Wasn't it you who suggested it?'

'Yes ... but might it not have just been *salt* water?'

She told him about the break-in at the church and the brine-filled font.

'It's easily big enough to drown someone in,' she said, 'and there's a splash of something on the rim. It looks like blood.'

'There was bruising on the body – signs of a struggle – but no lacerations.'

'Maybe the killer cut himself? Getting in the window? If you have a proper look, you might find more blood on the window or in the storeroom.'

'So—' Kevin sipped his coffee '—the killer broke into the church and made sure the door was open. Then he ... what? Just waited for Crowby to turn up?'

'That makes more sense than hauling a body up the cliff, doesn't it? He must have arranged to meet Crowby up there for some reason.' Liz looked at Kevin. 'What are you going to do now?'

'I'll go and take a look; then I'll talk to the boss.' He hesitated. 'If you don't mind, I won't mention you. She seems to have taken against you for some reason.'

Liz laughed. 'I can't imagine why.'

He gave her a penetrating look. 'Perhaps she doesn't like other people trying to do her job?'

'I can see how that would be irritating.'

He softened. 'But if this font thing turns out to be true, it's an important lead. Thank you.'

'You're welcome. But it's not the *how* that's important

though, is it? It's the *why*. Find that out, and we'll have our man.'

'We?'

'You.' Liz grinned. 'I mean *you'll* have your man.'

Kevin tried to keep a straight face and failed. 'Course you do!'

'What on earth was Crowby up to?' mused Liz. 'I wonder if there's anything missing.'

'Missing?'

'From the museum. Some of the exhibits must be pretty valuable, don't you think?'

'They haven't reported any thefts. And anyway—' Kevin drained his coffee '—I'm not sure it has anything to do with his work. We found letters in his cottage in White Horse Yard. Threatening letters.'

'Excellent! What did they say?'

'They were all along the lines of "I know what you're doing. It makes me sick. If you don't stop, I'll make you sorry you ever came to Whitby".'

'Cryptic.'

'Yeah. Could be talking about anything, really.'

'You're doing forensics, I suppose? On the letters?'

'Course.'

'Were they handwritten?'

'Laser printed.'

'It's still quite old-fashioned, though, isn't it? A letter. These days most blackmailers would just dash off an email and send it from an anonymous server. You're probably looking for someone older, not comfortable with technology.'

'Not necessarily,' said Kevin. 'I've been thinking about that. An email is very impersonal. There's no real sense of threat. It might just be someone who wanted to make more of an impact.'

Liz nodded. He had a point. 'Were they posted or hand-delivered?'

'No idea. Crowby hadn't kept the envelopes.'

'What on earth was he up to, I wonder.'

'That's the million-dollar question.' Kevin finished the last of his sausage roll and checked his watch. 'That and "why the hell do I do this job?" Catch up later, yeah?'

When he'd gone, Liz sat for a little while and finished the coffee, staring out to sea with Nelson at her feet.

There was definitely a storm coming in.

6

It hit the town in the early hours of the morning. Lightning flashed into Liz's bedroom in staccato bursts, and thunder rattled the roof windows. Nelson howled until Liz gave in and brought him upstairs. By the time the rain started, they were snuggled under the duvet, holding their breath together. Liz surrendered to sleep about an hour later, and when she woke up, the sun was shining. Only Nelson, snoring with his head on her pillow, was witness to the fact there had been a storm at all. Liz looked at her watch. Almost eight o'clock! She jumped out of bed.

'Come on, sleepyhead!' she called to Nelson. 'Ryan will be here any minute.'

The dog opened one eye, then closed it again. He looked supremely comfortable, which was probably why he hadn't woken up at his usual time of six thirty. Perhaps she should revise her strategy of making him sleep in the kitchen? She shook the thought away. They both needed their own space, even if it meant waking up ridiculously early.

. . .

RYAN ARRIVED SOON AFTERWARDS. It took him twenty-five minutes to fix the boiler, ten to check the gas stove, and another five to explain to her why she should never use the stove again. When he'd gone, Liz ignored her craving for a cup of tea by taking a shower. It was marvellous.

She'd arranged to meet Tilly at the café at nine thirty. As it was Tilly's day off, Tilly had agreed to accompany Liz to Chapel Antiques, to see what Wally Duguid had to say about her ginger beer bottles. After wrapping the bottles carefully in a scarf so they didn't clink together in the carrier bag, Liz said goodbye to Nelson and stepped out.

Mags had already opened the café when Liz arrived, so Liz had a coffee while she waited for Tilly to come down from the flat. It was almost ten when Tilly finally appeared, hair still wet from her shower.

'I doubt the shop opens 'til ten anyway,' she said by way of apology. 'Ohh, I'm so excited. It's ages since I had a really good rummage!' As the interior of the café showed, Tilly was a true magpie, attracted by anything shiny or out of the ordinary.

They set off to the other side of town. It was too early to be very busy, so Tilly was able to walk fast. Liz told her about her discovery with the font as she hurried to keep up with her.

'How did you know the water was salty?' asked Tilly.

'I tasted it. The Reverend caught me in the act.'

Tilly hooted with laughter.

'She said she ought to padlock the font, like they used to in olden days.'

'She probably should,' said Tilly. 'There's a market for it.'

'Eh?'

'Holy water. People sell it on eBay.'

'Who would want holy water?'

'I don't know. Witches? Vampire hunters?' Tilly dodged around a woman with a buggy. 'What did Kevin say?'

'He said he'd take a look.'

'It's a lot of trouble to go to, isn't it?'

Liz gave her a questioning look.

'Well, I mean, there are *much* easier ways of murdering someone. Stab them. Poison them. Strangle them. Garotte them.' Tilly was clearly on a roll. 'Suffocate them. Inject them. Hell's bells, you could just push them off the cliff, if it came to it. Why didn't they do that?'

Liz had given it some thought. 'I think it might be symbolic. Religious. Divine retribution?'

'Maybe ... Oh, here we are!'

They had arrived, Liz saw with surprise, at their destination. Chapel Antiques stood about halfway along Baxtergate, a shopping street that still retained some of its Victorian charm, but had been infected by modern commercialism. Olde worlde pubs rubbed shoulders with charity shops, bakers and chemists. As the name suggested, the antique shop had once been a church. It had an imposing red-brick façade with arched windows and steps leading up to the double door. A banner hanging on the railings said 'Browsers Welcome'.

'Looks promising.' Tilly leapt up the steps. Liz followed.

She wasn't sure what she was expecting, but it wasn't what she found inside. The interior of Chapel Antiques was cavernous, stuffed to the rafters with all kinds of furniture and artifacts. Dust motes drifted in the shafts of sunlight that slanted through the windows.

'Ohhhhh,' breathed Tilly. 'It's Aladdin's Cave!'

They went further in. It was quite hard to move between the shelves, as the floor was also stacked with stuff. Liz stubbed her toe on a dummy board painted to look like a pig, and almost knocked over a basket filled with antique door handles. As she caught the basket and pushed it upright, something else caught her eye – a bundle of fire pokers, forks and tongs. Liz pulled out one of the pokers. It was a lovely-looking thing, shiny brass, its handle formed into a ship in full sail.

'Oh ... my ... God!' Something had clearly caught Tilly's eye, too. Liz hurried to join her. All she could make out was something that looked like a collection of twigs, about the size of a pear.

'What is it?' she asked.

Tilly picked it up, her face shining with reverence. It was dusty and black, but looked suspiciously like a ...

'Hand of Glory,' breathed Tilly.

'A what?'

'The mummified hand of a criminal. Probably someone who was hung. It's supposed to give you special powers.'

'Ewww. Like what?'

'The ability to break into a house and steal things without being seen.' Tilly caught Liz's eye and gave a mischievous grin. 'Can you imagine?'

'Not really,' said Liz.

Tilly put the hand back on the shelf. 'I wonder what he wants for it. An arm and a leg, probably.' She realised what she'd said and giggled. 'An arm and a leg! Get it?'

Liz got it.

Tilly looked about. 'Is there anyone here, do you think?'

The shop floor seemed to be deserted, although it was hard to tell.

'Yoo-hoo!' called Tilly. 'YOOOOOO-HOOOOOO!'

They heard a door open somewhere in the bowels of the shop and then footsteps. A man stuck his head around a bookcase. He was heavily built, with a bowtie, beard and glasses.

'Can I be of assistance?'

Liz stepped forward. 'Mr Duguid? I called you yesterday, about the ginger beer bottles. Liz McLuckie.'

'Of course!' He pushed his glasses further up his nose. 'Just come through to the office.' He disappeared again behind the bookcase.

'I'm off to explore,' said Tilly. 'See you in a bit.'

Liz followed Duguid down a dusty corridor to the office, which was behind a half-glazed Victorian door that said laundry. It was surprisingly big inside, stacked with various antiques, including two large desks. A blonde woman sat at one of them in a fluffy pink top and full make-up, wielding a large tube of glue. She was trying to piece a broken jug back together.

'This is my wife, Myrtle,' said Duguid.

'Hello,' said Liz.

'Pleased to meet you,' said Myrtle. 'I don't suppose *you* know how to get Superglue out of mohair?'

'A pair of scissors?' suggested Liz.

Myrtle shuddered.

Wally Duguid glared at his wife, then looked meaningfully at the door. She sighed and stood up, smoothed her skirt over Marilyn Monroe curves, and headed out. As she passed her husband, Liz couldn't help but notice what a mismatched couple they were. Roger and Jessica Rabbit.

Duguid pushed his glasses back up his nose. 'Let's take a look, shall we?'

Liz took the bottles carefully out of the carrier bag and unwrapped them.

'You say you found them in an inglenook?'

'You wouldn't think so, would you? They look like new.'

'Hmmm.' His hand hovered briefly over the bigger bottle and then went to the smaller one. He picked it up to examine it.

'What do you think?' asked Liz.

'Not very valuable, I'm afraid. This one is quite common. I
have a few like it already. The larger bottle, with the ship, is a
little more unusual. More decorative, with local provenance. I
suppose it might attract a collector online.' He paused, thinking. 'I'll give you twenty pounds for the small one, and eighty
for the large.'

Liz tried to hide her disappointment. Duguid saw it and
gave a patronising smile. 'They might be Victorian, but they
were made in industrial quantities, I'm afraid. There's still a
lot of them about.'

'In such good condition?' She realised she still had the
poker. It had a price tag of twenty-five pounds on it. 'Tell you
what. How about we do a straight swap – the small bottle for
this poker. Taking into account the markup on both, I daresay
you'll still make a profit?'

Duguid thought about it, then nodded. 'And what about
the other one? Eighty pounds is a very fair price.'

She searched his face and saw the eagerness he was
trying to hide.

'I think I'll hold on to it for now.'

'How about ninety?'

'I'll think about it.'

Duguid watched as she wrapped the bottle up again in
the scarf and put it back into her bag with the poker. They
made their way back out to the showroom and found Tilly
and Myrtle with the grisly hand.

'This lady wants to know how much we want for the
Hand of Glory, Wally. There's no price on it.'

Duguid looked Tilly up and down, taking in the tattoos
and peroxide hair, and his expression tightened into something close to a sneer. 'Seven hundred.'

Tilly's face fell.

'If you know it's a Hand of Glory, you'll also know it's a

collector's item,' said Duguid. 'It should really be in a museum.'

'Then perhaps you should take better care of it,' suggested Liz. 'Rather than leave it collecting dust on a shelf out here.'

She steered Tilly out of the shop.

'Sorry, Tills. Seven hundred's a lot of money.'

'It is.' Tilly sighed. 'He was a bit of a dick about it, wasn't he?'

'A bit.'

'Did he buy your bottles?'

'I swapped the small one for a poker, but I kept the big one. He offered me ninety quid for it.'

'Not bad!'

'Maybe,' said Liz. 'But I've a feeling it's worth more.'

7

Liz spent the rest of the weekend clearing rubble out of the inglenook. On Monday, she took Nelson back up to St Mary's churchyard. All that remained of the police investigation was a flutter of crime scene tape tied to a metal stake at the spot she'd found Ian Crowby's body. Nelson lifted his leg against it. There was no sign of rabbits, so Liz decided to take Nelson through to the abbey grounds, where he might have better luck. It would cost her a couple of pounds to get in, and dogs weren't technically allowed, but Frida, the young woman who worked in the ticket office, was a dog lover. As long as the abbey wasn't too busy, and Liz had poop bags with her, Frida would turn a blind eye to Liz sneaking him under the barrier.

As it happened, they got nowhere near the ticket office. They'd just gone through the gate into the car park, and Liz was just about to clip Nelson onto his lead, when she spotted Dora Spackle halfway across the tarmac, headed for the museum gate. Dora and Nelson saw each other at the same time. They both froze. Nelson growled, low in his throat, and shot off towards her.

'Shit!' Liz went icy with horror.

There was no way Dora was going to make it.

To her credit, she could move pretty fast for a woman in advanced middle age, but Nelson was closer to her than she was to the museum gate. Luckily, when he reached her, he didn't tackle her to the ground, but just hurled himself in front of her, so he stood between her and the gate. He growled, hackles up.

Liz caught up with them.

'Call your bloody dog off!' shouted Dora. 'He's a menace!' Her face was bright red. She clutched her handbag to her heaving tweed bosom.

Liz managed to put Nelson on his lead. 'I'm so sorry, Dora.'

'I should call the police!'

Liz wasn't going to take that lying down. 'In fairness, he wouldn't be like this if you hadn't kicked him at Christmas.'

'He ate my handbag!'

That was true. But still. 'There was no need to kick him.'

'Just get him away from me.'

Now he was back on the lead, Nelson had stopped growling and was ignoring Dora completely, as if nothing had happened. Liz tied him to the railing a safe distance away. She saw that Dora had dropped something on her sprint, and went to pick it up. It was a glove. An odd thing to wear in June, but Dora was an odd woman. Liz returned it to her.

'You dropped this. Are you okay?'

Dora was still trying to get her breath back. Her fringe had escaped from the art deco clip she habitually wore, and her glasses were fogged. To Liz's surprise, she saw her eyes were wet.

'Why don't we sit down for a minute?' There was a bench at the museum gate. Dora allowed Liz to steer her to it, and pushed her fringe back into her hair clip with a shaking hand.

'I'm not usually so ...' She tailed off, embarrassed. 'It's been a terrible week.'

Of course.

'The professor,' said Liz. 'It must have been a shock.'

'That's one way of putting it.' Dora sniffed. 'It's been a horrible inconvenience. Police everywhere. People asking questions.'

'He worked with you, didn't he, last summer?'

'If you can call it that.' Dora pulled the glove on and took a tissue from her bag. 'He came for a few weeks, dangled around making a nuisance of himself, and then buggered off again. Complete waste of time.'

'What was he helping you with?'

'He was *supposed* to be helping us archive the stuff too delicate to display. Take photographs, pack them safely, make a record of their current condition, that kind of thing. I had it covered anyway. I didn't need "supervising".' She made ironic speech marks in the air as she said it. 'I have just as much experience as he has.' She corrected herself. 'Had.'

Tears welled again, and she dabbed at them with her tissue.

'I suppose everything is still where it should be?' asked Liz.

'What?'

'In the museum. All the exhibits. There's nothing missing?'

Dora's eyes sharpened. 'Why should there be?'

'I don't know. I was just wondering.'

'Of course there's nothing missing!' Dora got to her feet and pulled herself up to her full height. 'I have everything perfectly under control. Like I always do.' She looked down at Liz, outraged. 'I hope you're not suggesting I can't do my job?'

'Of course not. I just ...'

Dora stalked off, throwing one last glare at Nelson as she let herself through the museum gate. She stomped down the path, forcing two museum visitors to leap out of her way. Liz watched her go in disbelief. Dora Spackle was a hard woman to like – anyone in the town would tell you that – but every time Liz came across her, she couldn't quite believe *how* hard.

WHEN SHE GOT HOME, she set to work cleaning up the dust in the kitchen created by her grand inglenook reveal. Every time she wiped a surface, the dust rose and resettled, so she had to wipe every surface several times. When she vacuumed the carpet, she had to empty the bag twice. It took a couple of hours to make the kitchen respectable, or at least as respectable as she could make it without ripping everything out and having it refitted. Then she made herself a cup of tea with the electric kettle she'd bought after her visit to the antique shop in Baxtergate.

She sat in her armchair, sipping her tea, and took a good look around. She was beginning to wish she hadn't started the work in Kipper Cottage, but had stuck to her original plan of doing up Gull Cottage first. Then, at least, she'd be able to shut the door on the mess and live in relatively hygienic conditions. She promised herself that she would only restore the inglenook in Kipper – so she could light a fire – and then go back to plan A. She took another sip of her tea and saw that the corner of the carpet she'd lifted the day before was still sticking up. She put her tea down and went to tug on it a bit more. After a few minutes, she'd managed to rip it up another couple of inches, past the hearth, so she could see beneath. Not only the hearth, but the whole floor was stone – maybe even the original flags. Unfortunately the carpet, like the wall cladding, was stuck down with glue. She might eventually be able to take the carpet up, but had no idea if the glue would ever come off. If the stone was porous, it probably wouldn't. A disheartening thought.

She finished her tea and took another shower. Then she heated herself a microwave meal. With the microwave and the electric kettle, she could manage without the stove for now, but would have to think about what she was going to replace it with.

She really liked the look of Agas, but didn't know much about them and imagined they would be hard to cook on – probably not a good idea for a holiday rental. Perhaps she could get a modern gas or electric stove with the same kind of vintage look? She went upstairs to the sitting room, found her laptop in the bureau, and switched it on. As she did, she tried not to look at her surroundings. The sitting room had the same faux-wood cladding as the kitchen, and the same horrible swirly carpet. There was no gas fire – no heating of any kind, in fact – although there was probably a chimney breast somewhere under the cladding. It wasn't likely to be an inglenook, though.

Liz brought herself back to the present. One thing at a time. Stoves.

It took her a little while to find what she was looking for, but she eventually discovered a manufacturer who made electric ranges that looked very like Agas. The plates and the oven were individually controllable. Perfect. Not a bad price either, although, of course, she would have to buy two. As she bookmarked the page, another thought occurred to her.

She went onto eBay and typed ANTIQUE GINGER BEER BOTTLES into the search bar. There was quite a lot. Realising she'd have to narrow it down, she added WHITBY to the search. Half a dozen listings came up, all similar to the first bottle she'd swapped for the poker. Except one. One with a picture of a sailing ship, almost exactly the same as her bigger bottle, but not in such good condition. She looked at the Buy it Now price. Then looked again. Five hundred pounds! She *knew* Wally Duguid had been trying to rip her off!

A BANGING NOISE from downstairs made Liz jump. It was followed by the sound of barking. She scrambled down the stairs to see who was at the door. Nelson was beside himself, barking and snarling. Liz managed to wrestle him into the understairs cupboard, and the whole staircase shook as he battered himself against the door. What on earth had got him into such a frenzy?

She had her answer when she opened the front door. Dora Spackle stood on the step, nose red and eyes swollen with tears. Liz stared at her in shock.

'There *is* something missing from the museum,' she sobbed. 'Something very valuable.'

Liz was speechless.

'I didn't know who else to turn to,' stuttered Dora. 'Can you help me?'

8

Dora eyed the mug of tea Liz gave her as if it might have poison in it. Even when she was red-eyed and begging for help, she could still manage to be objectionable. They'd taken their tea up to the sitting room so Nelson couldn't hear Dora's voice. Liz could hear him thrashing about in the cupboard downstairs, but didn't dare let him out. Hopefully he would settle.

Dora sniffed and took a sip of her tea.

'What you said in the car park made me worry.' She gave Liz an accusing look. 'I couldn't imagine there would be anything missing in the archives, but thought I should check, just in case.' Her eyes welled with tears. 'And ... it's gone!'

'What is?' Liz stifled her irritation.

'St Ælfflaed's girdle! Our most valuable artifact.' Dora looked at Liz as if she was expecting some kind of reaction, but Liz looked at her blankly.

'Who's St Ælfflaed?' she asked.

Dora's eyes opened wide. 'The Abbess of Whitby. One of our most famous abbesses. Surely you've heard of her?'

Liz shook her head.

'She was a friend of St Cuthbert. You've heard of *him*, I suppose?'

'Of course.' Cuthbert was one of Northern England's best-known saints and was buried in Durham Cathedral.

'The girdle was a gift to Ælfflaed from Cuthbert.'

'If you don't mind me saying so, a girdle seems a strange present for a monk to give a nun.'

Dora rolled her eyes. 'Not a girdle as *we* know it. Not underwear. A medieval girdle is a belt worn on the outside of a kirtle.'

'Oh.'

'It was embroidered with flowers and birds. A beautiful thing, although the colours had faded over the centuries, and the cloth was rather frayed. It was very, very fragile. And very valuable. It was insured for more than eighty thousand pounds.'

'Ooof,' said Liz.

Dora ignored her. 'I hope the thief is taking care of it.'

'You don't think it was Crowby, then?'

Dora was astonished. 'Professor Crowby? Why on earth would *he* take it?'

Liz thought it was obvious. 'Didn't you say it's valuable?'

'It is. But it's worth so much more than money. Historically speaking, it's irreplaceable. Ian ... Professor Crowby ... knew that. He might not have been the best archivist, but he would never have been crass enough to consider the girdle in purely monetary terms.'

'Did he have any contact with it while he was with you?'

Dora nodded. 'We couldn't display the girdle in its current condition. It's far too fragile. But the museum trustees were keen to have it on display to the public. The professor helped me take it out of the archive to check its condition and photograph it so we could assess how best to stabilise it for display.'

'I take it the archive's usually locked?'

Dora burst into fresh tears.

'Not always. I ... I ...' She really was distraught.

Liz took pity on her. 'Don't blame yourself.'

'I don't!' Dora glared at her. 'I blame whoever stole the girdle! I hope God strikes them dead!'

Okay.

'Is there CCTV in the museum?' asked Liz.

'Only in the gift shop.'

Of course, thought Liz. *Because cheap reproduction jewellery and postcards are so much more valuable than priceless medieval relics.*

'Who else had access to the archives?'

'Any of the museum staff. Or even a visitor ... someone could have wandered in when the door was unlocked.' Dora pushed her fringe back into her hair clip and sniffed. 'Actually, I think I know who the thief is.'

'Oh?'

'Niall Fitzgerald.' She wiped her nose. 'He's an archaeologist, doing a dig on some of our Saxon graves. He wants to go to Athens. I think he took the girdle to pay for a place on a dig there. Maybe he killed the professor, too!'

Liz was finding it hard to keep up with Dora's scattered accusations. 'Why would he do that?'

'Because the professor had just found out Fitzgerald's degree is bogus, and was about to tell the trustees. Perhaps he killed the professor *and* took the girdle!'

It all sounded a bit convoluted to Liz. If Dora knew the degree was bogus, surely it wouldn't help Fitzgerald for him to kill Crowby? One thing was clear. 'You have to tell the police.'

'I can't.' Dora shook her head. Although she'd *said* she didn't blame herself for not keeping the archive secure, she clearly didn't want to tell anyone but Liz that she hadn't done.

It made her look bad at her job, which Liz suspected was the worst thing that could possibly happen to her.

'I don't understand why you've come to me,' said Liz.

'Help me confront Fitzgerald. We can make him confess.'

Liz could just imagine it: Two middle-aged ladies rough-housing a full-grown man. Her thoughts must have shown on her face.

'He's not very big,' said Dora. 'Just a boy, really.'

Liz laughed. She couldn't help it.

'I don't see what's funny.' Dora glared at her.

'Sorry.' As Liz tried to straighten her face, a thought occurred. She and Dora were hardly friends. Dora must have no one else she could turn to for help. A sad thought.

'I might have known *you* wouldn't take this seriously,' snapped Dora.

Liz almost laughed again. Really, the woman made it impossible to have any sympathy for her.

'Listen.' Liz took Dora's empty mug from her and set it firmly on the table. 'I can't help you. If the girdle is as valuable as you say it is, you have to tell the police. It might be connected in some way with the professor's murder, or it might not. Either way, it isn't something you should deal with on your own.'

Dora put her hands over her face.

'I don't think I can bear it,' she muttered.

'You'll have to. If you want the police to have any chance of getting the girdle back.'

'But the police are horrible. That awful woman!'

Liz didn't need to be Sherlock Holmes to deduce she was talking about Inspector Flint.

'They're not all bad,' said Liz. 'In fact, I know a very nice one.'

· · ·

WHILE KEVIN and Dora were having a 'chat' in her sitting room, Liz freed Nelson from the cupboard and took him out. They went up the abbey steps as the sun was setting. From the top, the old town looked picture-perfect in the rosy light. Liz took a deep breath of salt air and thanked her lucky stars she was able to live in such a stunning place. A stunning and *interesting* place. Things certainly hadn't been boring lately!

On impulse, rather than take Nelson into the churchyard, Liz decided to go into the abbey grounds. It was officially closed that time of the evening, the ticket office shuttered and empty, but Liz clambered over the metal turnstile, while Nelson squeezed through underneath. It was something they'd often done before.

They had the abbey grounds completely to themselves. As soon as Liz unclipped Nelson's lead, he darted off to explore. The parts of the abbey that were still standing – the walls of the nave and the soaring eastern wall – had a gaunt, iconic beauty, easily recognisable from all the tourist litera-ture of the town. Most of the rest of the ruins were little more than foundations, barely knee high, scattered over the clifftop and enclosed by a high boundary wall. The site had started in the seventh century as a Christian monastery for men and women, and had turned into one of the most important reli-gious centres in Britain, a hub of learning and culture. Britain's very first poet, Caedmon, had worked there as a shepherd. On still evenings like this, alone in the grounds, Liz liked to imagine she could hear medieval plainsong drifting across the clifftop, the voices of men and women lifted in harmony, praising the Lord. Liz listened. And listened again. She *could* hear something. Not plainsong, but a whistled tune: 'The Girl from Ipanema'?

She followed the sound around to the other side of the abbey ruins and spotted a large tent pitched against the northern boundary wall. It was more of a tarpaulin than a tent, really, about three metres wide, with two of its sides rolled up. There was a stack of muddy sieves, buckets and a fishing stool beside it. The whistling was coming from inside. Liz went to investigate.

A young man lay flat on his back next to a shallow rectangular hole. He was dressed in shorts and a Hawaiian shirt, alternately whistling and taking a drag on a rolled cigarette. By the acrid scent that hung in the air, Liz thought it wasn't just tobacco.

'Evening,' she said.

He shrieked and leapt to his feet. Liz saw he was young – probably early twenties – with a mop of black hair and very blue eyes. She guessed she was looking at Niall Fitzgerald, the man Dora suspected of stealing the girdle.

'Christ on a bike!' He clapped his muddy hand to his heart. 'Why would you creep up on a man like that?' He nipped out his joint surreptitiously and flicked it out of the tent. Liz pretended not to see.

'I didn't mean to give you a fright,' she said. 'I just wondered what you were doing over here.'

'Good question.' He pulled a face. 'One I ask myself every day. I'm working on some of the Saxon graves. The locals think I'm digging up skeletons, but mostly it's just muck and bits of iron. Come and take a look if you like.'

Liz stepped into the tent and followed him to a table. It was laid out with a dozen or so shards of metal, each one about an inch long, encrusted in mud and rust.

'Coffin nails. The wood and bones in the graves are long gone. Just stains in the mud.' He picked something up and showed it to Liz.

'My most exciting find to date.'

It was a piece of bone, with marks scratched onto the surface. 'Not Saxon, obviously,' he said.

'Scrimshaw?'

He nodded. 'Part of a pipe. Most likely mid-eighteenth century. The name's Niall, by the way.' He offered her his hand, but saw the mud on it and dropped it again.

'Liz McLuckie,' she said. 'Pleased to meet you. I can't imagine it's been easy lately, with all the rain we've been having?'

'You can say that again. I thought Ireland was wet, but this place.' He shook his head. 'This place is a feckin' nightmare.'

Liz smiled. It wasn't the most tactful thing to say to a local. She suspected his cigarettes were at least partly responsible for the indiscretion.

Her phone buzzed.

'Excuse me.' It was a text from Kevin.

ALL DONE HERE.

She turned to Niall. 'Got to go,' she said. 'I'll let you get on with … whatever it was you were doing.' They grinned at each other, remembering how she'd found him.

'Hang on, and I'll come down with you. I'm finished for the night.'

He grabbed a rucksack, let the tent flaps down and tied them. As he was putting on his rucksack, he saw her doubtful glance at the tent.

'Not very secure, I know,' he said. 'But really there's nothing worth nicking. Unless someone really, *really* needs a rusty bucket.'

As they made their way towards the gate, they were joined by Nelson, muddy and panting from his persecution of the rabbit population. He gave Niall the once-over and decided to ignore him.

'How long are you going to be here?' Liz asked Niall.

He shrugged. 'A few weeks? I still have one grave to excavate, but it depends on the weather.'

They both clambered over the turnstile while Nelson squeezed underneath.

'Do you often finish this late?' she asked him.

'Depends. If it's dry, I'll keep going. It doesn't happen very often. I'd like to go somewhere warm next, but to get a place on a really exciting dig costs money.'

Liz was surprised. 'I thought they paid *you*?'

'Some do, yeah. Like this one. But there's still airfare and accommodation to cover. Others aren't paid at all. You do them for the *craic*, and because it looks good on your CV.'

'How much does it cost?'

'Depends on the dig. The one I have my eye on in Athens is paid for, but the airfare is three hundred quid. Ma would help out if she could, but ...' He tailed off miserably. 'When I'm done here, I'll probably have to go back to Dublin. Get a bar job.'

Liz realised that might happen sooner rather than later if his degree really *was* bogus. She couldn't imagine Dora keeping that to herself.

They parted company at the bottom of the steps. She watched him wander off – a bedraggled, muddy figure in walking boots and a Hawaiian shirt. He seemed an unlikely thief and murderer.

9

The next day, after walking Nelson, Liz spent the morning trying to peel her fitted carpet from the stone floor in the kitchen. Progress was painfully slow. She had to use all her strength to lift the carpet enough to slide a craft knife underneath so she could cut it free from the glue. It was rather like shearing a sheep, but much, much slower, and harder on the knees. While she worked, she thought about the girdle.

In her opinion, Crowby was still the most likely thief. He had been in contact with it, knew how to get it, and knew what it was worth. In spite of what Dora had said, money was the obvious motive.

Where was the girdle now? No one knew exactly when it had been taken: It had been ten months since Dora had put it back in the archive. Crowby could have sold it already. Maybe online? If there was a market for holy water, there was bound to be a market for other religious relics. After a few moments, Liz rejected that idea. The girdle was too well known to be sold openly. If someone did try to sell it online, they wouldn't be able to give the girdle's full provenance, which would seriously reduce the amount someone would be prepared to pay for it. Perhaps Crowby had shady black-market contacts? If so, had they killed him for the girdle? People had been murdered for a lot less than eighty thousand pounds.

THAT AFTERNOON, Liz went shopping. Her list was somewhat eclectic – almonds, apricots, a pig's ear, a litre of rubbing alcohol and a packet of blades for her craft knife. She'd broken all the blades she had on the stubborn carpet and still had only lifted about a third of it. The alcohol was to try to dissolve the glue residue on the stone floor. The pig's ear was Nelson's favourite treat, to make up for his incarceration the previous day.

Luckily, her shopping didn't take long – you could buy almost anything in the town if you knew where to look. As Liz passed Chapel Antiques, she saw Myrtle Duguid coming out. She would have waved at her, but her hands were full of shopping bags, so she nodded instead. Myrtle, dressed in a pink velour tracksuit, looked right through her. After an initial flash of dismay at being ignored, Liz forgave Myrtle. Really, she'd hardly met her for five minutes in the antique shop, so it was hardly surprising she didn't remember her.

As she hauled her shopping over the swing bridge into the old town, a thought occurred. Kevin had said Ian Crowby owned a cottage in White Horse Yard. Could it hurt to take a look? She might not be able to tell which one was his, but at least it would satisfy her curiosity. Instead of turning down Sandgate as she usually did, she carried on a little bit further to Church Street. The cobbled stretch of shops from the main road to the Old Town Hall wasn't one she often walked, as it was always very busy. About halfway along stood the White Horse and Griffin, an ancient coaching inn, now a popular pub. The pub was no wider than its doorway at the front, but it went back a long way and broadened out at the back. Beside the pub entrance was the narrow tunnel to White Horse Yard. Liz was just about to turn into it, when she had to jump aside for someone coming out.

'Oh, it's you,' said Dora Spackle.

'Hello. How are you? I didn't really get the chance to ask you how things went with Kevin the other night?'

'Well enough.' Was it Liz's imagination, or did Dora look very uncomfortable? Dora said nothing more, but just stomped off, leaving Liz standing on the pavement with her mouth open.

Still slightly stunned, and vowing never to get involved in any of Dora's dramas again, Liz went into the tunnel. White Horse Yard was where the stables of the coaching inn used to be, and it was now one of the most sought-after locations for cottages in the old town. The tunnel, which was about twenty feet long, was narrow and dark, but opened out into a pleasant cobbled yard surrounded by half a dozen cottages. Even further back there was a little drying green and a collection of tiny gardens – a rare thing in Whitby old town. The cottages commanded high prices as holiday lets and rarely came on the market. The professor had done well to buy one. But which one was it?

It occurred to Liz she must look very conspicuous, standing there with her shopping bags. She looked around and tried to guess which cottage had been the professor's. Two had buckets and spades by the doors, freshly covered in sand, and another had a bicycle standing outside. Another two had key safes by the doors – a sure sign of holiday lets.

That left just one, which showed no signs of life at all. Liz went to the window and peered inside. It clearly hadn't been occupied for some time, but was very tidy. Which was odd, because she assumed the police had searched the cottage after finding Crowby's body.

'Can I help you?' A young woman stuck her head out of the cottage next door, the one with the bicycle.

Liz flushed scarlet. She didn't know what to say. 'Yes ... I'm ... um ... looking for Professor Crowby.'

'Oh.' The young woman's face crumpled.

Liz went to join her. She could see her eyes were red, and her skin was blotchy. She'd clearly been crying.

'Are you okay?' Liz asked.

'Yes. No. Actually, I think you'd better come in.' She ushered Liz in through the door, which led directly into the living room. 'Please, have a seat.'

Liz put her bags down and perched on the edge of an overstuffed floral armchair.

'I'm the professor's daughter, Janet. I'm sorry to have to tell you, but my father died a few days ago.'

'Oh.'

'I'm surprised you haven't read about it. Or seen it on the news.'

Liz shook her head. She felt awful. She hated having told the lie, even if it was by omission, but it was too late now to admit the truth.

'I'm really very sorry,' said Liz. 'I didn't mean to disturb you.'

'It's quite alright.' Janet wiped her face. Apart from the signs of tears, she was pleasant-featured, with bobbed red hair. 'It's been something of a morning for visitors.'

Liz wondered if she was talking about Dora Spackle.

'How did you know my father?' asked Janet.

Liz had to think fast. 'I didn't. Not really. But I heard he's an antiques expert, and I had a couple of things I wondered if he could take a look at.' Not too far from the truth. One truth, anyway.

'He probably would have been able to help you. As you can see, he loved antiques.' She was talking about the room, which was furnished exclusively with old furniture. Much of it looked expensive, with inlaid marquetry and gilding. It looked a bit odd in a fisherman's cottage, but Liz made an appreciative noise.

'I'd help you if I could,' said Janet, 'but I know nothing about antiques.'

'Not to worry.' Liz realised she hadn't introduced herself. 'I'm Liz McLuckie, by the way.'

They shook hands.

'Would you like a cup of tea?'

Liz hesitated. She didn't want to stay there under false pretences, but also didn't want to be rude. She shook her head. 'I don't want to intrude any more than I already have.'

'Not at all. In fact, I'd be glad of the company. It's very strange being in here without ... on my own.'

Liz thought for an uncomfortable moment that Janet was about to cry again. Luckily, the moment passed.

'In that case, yes, I'd love a cup.' She couldn't really refuse.

Janet disappeared into the kitchen.

'I won't be a minute,' she called back. 'The kettle's just boiled.'

Liz used the opportunity to have a proper look around. As well as the antiques and the chair she was sitting on, there was a comfortable two-seater sofa, a black lacquer coffee table and a modern TV on the wall. Everything was very tidy, but Liz supposed that Janet must have tidied up after the police had searched the cottage. Liz crept over to take a look at the photographs on the bookcase. They were mostly of Janet, including one that looked like a graduation photo. The single one that wasn't of Janet showed a tall man shaking hands with Prince Philip. Liz recognised Ian Crowby from photos she'd seen of him in the local news. It was hard to believe it was the same man she'd found lying face down in the churchyard.

As well as photos, there was a collection of vintage knick-knacks – a pair of small crystal candlesticks, a ship in a bottle and a tortoiseshell hairbrush and mirror. Liz looked at the hairbrush ... and looked again.

'That was taken at the Queen's Garden Party a few years ago,' said Janet, emerging from the kitchen. She placed the tray she was carrying on the coffee table. 'Prince Philip was very interested in Dad's work at Windsor Castle. Would you like milk?'

'Please.' Liz sat down again and watched as Janet poured tea into two dainty cups. 'It must be very hard for you just now.'

Janet sighed. 'Not as hard as it is for my mum.' She saw Liz's surprise. 'They separated a couple of years ago, but they were talking about getting back together again.' She handed Liz her cup. 'I don't think she'll ever get over it.'

'Your dad lived here alone?'

Janet nodded. 'He moved in last year when he was working with some of the Whitby museums. I suppose he thought it would be handy being on the doorstep.'

Judging by the blonde hairs Liz had spotted in the hairbrush, she suspected there could be another reason too, but kept that thought to herself. She drank her tea as quickly as she could without seeming rude.

'Just look at all this stuff.' Janet sighed. 'It'll take me an age to clear out. Luckily, one of dad's friends is an antique dealer.'

'Not Wally Duguid?'

'Yes. Do you know him?'

'Not really.' She knew he was a chancer, but she could hardly say that to Janet. She just hoped he wouldn't rip her off. She quickly changed the subject. 'If you need a cleaner when you're done, I know a very good one. Iris Gladwell.'

'That would be really useful, thank you. I work full time and have kids, so ...' She shrugged.

Liz felt very sorry for her. Her own parents had been dead for quite a while. Her father had died first, and then after her mum's death, clearing out her flat in Edinburgh had been a mammoth task. It wasn't just the physical effort, but the mental toll it took, handling things her mum had been attached to. And, of course, Janet also had the added strain that her father had been murdered. Liz couldn't imagine what that must be like, being the centre of so much speculation.

Janet rummaged in her cardigan pocket and brought out a card, which she gave to Liz. It was a business card, with Janet's name and contact number on it. Janet Masters – Macmillan Nurse, Cancer Support. The young woman went up even more in Liz's estimation.

'Ask Iris to call me when she gets the chance,' said Janet.

'I will.' Liz put the card in her own pocket. 'And if you need anything, anything at all, just give me a call. I'm in the phone book. The only McLuckie in Whitby.'

10

'When you're finished those,' said Benedict, 'you can chop the coriander if you don't mind? Kev, pass it to Liz, will you? It's in the carrier bag on the floor.'

Kevin did as instructed and tossed Liz a small paper bag. She put the almonds she'd chopped into a bowl and started on the coriander.

Benedict stirred his tagine, which had been bubbling on the stove for some time, filling the kitchen with the delicious aroma of North African spices. Kevin was wrapping the pitta bread in foil, ready to go in the oven. Liz smiled as she chopped. She wasn't a good cook – pretty appalling, in fact – but she was a very efficient kitchen skivvy. Give her a sharp knife and a mountain of veggies to prepare and she was in her element. Mark had always been the cook. He had been a wizard in the kitchen, rarely working from a recipe, but combining flavours and judging quantities and timings instinctively. His Sunday roasts were spectacular. He and Liz would spend an hour or so preparing everything in advance, then pop out to the pub for a quick drink while the meat was in the oven. Returning home, they'd be greeted by the delicious scent of roasted meat and would have nothing else to do but turn on the veggies and open a bottle of wine.

The sound of someone clearing his throat brought Liz back to the present. Benedict was looking at her with concern. She realised that she'd stopped chopping, and her eyes were wet. She wiped them quickly.

'Coriander,' she said to Benedict. 'It does that to me sometimes.'

'Would you like me to take over?'

'No, it's fine. I'll be done in a sec.'

Benedict nodded and moved back to the stove. 'How are you doing with that pitta, Kev?'

The question was ironic, because Kevin had abandoned the flatbread only half-wrapped and was engrossed in the local evening paper – the *Whitby Bugle* – that he'd picked up from the counter.

'Bloody hell,' he said. 'Flint's going to wring Donnie Satterthwaite's neck.'

'Why?' asked Liz. Donald Satterthwaite was one of the local reporters who worked on the *Bugle*.

'He says here that Ian Crowby was drowned. How the hell did he find that out?'

'You can't keep anything a secret in Whitby,' said Benedict.

'True,' said Liz. 'How's the investigation going, anyway?'

'Slowly.' Kevin looked glum. 'No real leads. We've been looking into Crowby's finances.' He went back to the newspaper and started to read again.

Liz felt a flash of irritation. 'And?' she prompted.

Kevin grinned. Liz realised he'd been teasing her.

'Well,' he said, 'strangely for someone who was pretty well paid, his finances were a mess.'

'Really?' Liz's curiosity was piqued. 'What kind of mess?'

'I can't give you details.'

'I won't tell anyone.' She drew a cross over her heart. 'Cross my heart and hope to die.'

'It'll be *me* who dies if Flint finds out.' He saw her crestfallen expression. 'Let's just say he had expensive tastes. The only thing keeping him afloat were PayPal payments into his account. We're trying to trace where they've come from.'

'And what about the threatening notes?' asked Liz. 'Any leads on those?'

Kevin shook his head. 'No prints or anything at all on them. The paper is just bog-standard printer paper from a supermarket.'

'And the blood in the church?'

'Gone to the lab. But it looks as if you might be right about the font. There were abrasions on Crowby's face that could have come from the chancel steps.'

Benedict finished wrapping the pitta bread in foil and slid it into the oven.

'Tilly's late,' he said. 'Even for her. Anyone seen her at all today?'

'She wasn't in the café this afternoon when I gave Janet Masters's business card to Iris.'

Kevin looked at her sharply. 'Janet Masters? As in Professor Crowby's daughter, Janet Masters?'

'Mm.' Liz tried to look innocent. 'She's looking for a cleaner.'

'I didn't know you knew her,' said Kevin.

'We met a couple of days ago.'

'That's a coincidence.'

Liz made a noncommittal noise. 'Want a hand to set the table, Benedict?'

Tilly still hadn't arrived when the tagine was ready.

'We can't leave it much longer,' said Benedict, 'or everything will dry out.'

They decided to go ahead and eat without her. The tagine was as delicious as it smelled, rich and spicy, with just the right hint of sweetness from the apricots Liz had brought. They'd just finished and were starting to clear the table when the doorbell rang.

'About time!' Benedict went to answer it. A minute later, Tilly stomped into the kitchen, pink-faced and fuming. Benedict followed, looking worried.

'Late as usual,' said Kevin, oblivious. 'Where have you been?'

Tilly glared at him and folded her arms. 'As if you don't know.'

'Eh?'

'I've been in the bloody police station, that's where! For the last three hours!'

Kevin couldn't have looked more astonished. 'What are you talking about?'

'Your boss. She turned up at the café with a search warrant, then hauled me in to "help with enquiries". Something about a theft from the museum?'

'The girdle,' said Liz.

'The *what*?'

'Not a *girdle* girdle,' said Kevin. 'Some medieval relic to do with the abbey.'

Tilly wrestled her cardigan off and dropped into a chair. Benedict poured her a glass of wine as the others gathered round her.

'Flint must have found out about my convictions for breaking and entering,' she said. She gulped her wine. For a second, Liz could see the fear beneath the bravado.

'Don't worry,' said Kevin. 'I'll tell her she's barking up the wrong tree.' He hesitated. 'As long as ...'

'As long as ...?'

'As long as you *didn't* have anything to do with it?'

Everyone stared at him.

'Kev,' began Benedict, 'I really don't think …'

'No offence, Tills,' cut in Kevin. He looked uncomfortable, but was clearly determined to see it through. 'I've often heard you say you miss the excitement.'

Tilly sighed. 'I *do* miss it.' She turned to Benedict. 'It's okay, B, I can see why he had to ask. I really can. But I'm not stupid enough to risk everything I have with Mags for a bloody medieval … whatever it was.'

'A girdle,' said Liz.

Kevin looked relieved. 'I'll have a word with Flint in the morning.'

'Thanks.' Tilly still looked dubious. 'I have to say, though, she doesn't seem open to persuasion. As I was leaving the station, she told me she knew I was the thief, and it was only a matter of time before she proved it.'

That really worried Liz. She couldn't imagine Flint backing off Tilly easily.

'Maybe the best way to get you off the hook,' she suggested, 'is to put someone else *on* it.'

'What do you mean?' asked Benedict.

'I mean we should find out who *really* took the girdle.'

Kevin eyed her nervously.

Liz continued. 'My money's on Crowby. I think he stole it, and then someone else killed him for it. Problem is, we'd have to prove it.'

'I'd love to see Flint's face if we caught the real thief,' said Tilly. 'Ohhh … we might even catch the murderer, too!'

Now Kevin looked *really* alarmed. 'It's one thing to *speculate* about who might have murdered Ian Crowby, but another thing entirely to involve yourselves in the investigation. You're not professionals, and you could really mess things up. It might even be dangerous.'

'You always were a spoilsport,' sniffed Tilly, 'even at school.'

It was clear from her dismissive tone that Kevin hadn't made himself clear. He tried again.

'This is me officially telling you both' – he looked pointedly at Tilly and Liz – 'in my professional capacity as a police officer, *not* to get involved. Okay?'

Tilly looked at Liz and raised her eyebrows.

Kevin persisted. 'Okay, Tills?'

Tilly turned to Benedict. 'Is there any food left, B? I'm starving.'

AFTER TILLY HAD EATEN, it was too late to start a game of mah-jong, so they packed up the table and agreed to turn up earlier the following week.

Benedict helped Liz with her coat at the door. She stepped outside.

'Liz?'

'Mm?' She was preoccupied with thoughts of Ian Crowby and the girdle.

'Grief's a funny thing,' he said. His expression was gentle. 'It has no expiry date. It has a habit of ambushing you when you least expect it.'

She realised he was talking about her tears earlier, when they were making dinner. She glanced at Kevin and Tilly. They were halfway up the garden path and couldn't hear them.

'I know,' she said. She couldn't think what else to say, uncomfortable with the sudden intimacy between them.

'I go to a grief support group every Saturday night. It's been very helpful for me, and it might help you too. You can come with me if you like, whenever you want.'

She looked up into his eyes and saw the genuine concern

there. A support group wasn't really her thing – she'd be reluctant to air her private woes in public – but she didn't want to disappoint Benedict or make him think she wasn't grateful.

'That's good to know,' she said. 'Thank you. I'll think about it.'

SHE DID THINK ABOUT IT. She thought about it off and on all through the night as she drifted in and out of sleep. It wasn't so much the idea of the support group that kept her awake – she doubted she would go – but the fact that Benedict had wanted her to go in the first place. Either it meant he felt comfortable enough with her to open up about his grief, or that she barely registered enough for it to matter whether he opened up or not. She tossed and turned. She knew she was overthinking it, but couldn't seem to help herself.

As the night wore on, she became aware that something else was keeping her awake. Her left knee was starting to ache. By three o' clock it had turned from an ache to a throb, and she was forced to get up and fetch some painkillers from the bathroom cabinet. As she hobbled back to bed, she cursed the kitchen carpet. She'd been on her knees down there for three days straight, ripping the bloody thing up. It was hardly surprising her middle-aged body was rebelling. How could she even think about starting a physical relationship at her age? She stopped, realising what she'd just thought. Until that moment, she hadn't been aware she felt that way about Benedict.

It really, really shocked her.

11

Liz felt she'd only been asleep a few minutes when her canine alarm clock woke her up. She groaned as she rolled out of bed and tried to put her weight on her left leg. She didn't know whether it was the painkillers or the fact she'd been horizontal for a couple of hours, but her knee did seem a bit better. She hobbled downstairs to feed Nelson. Ever since Dora Spackle had turned up on her doorstep, he'd been restless and on edge. He was giving the cupboard under the stairs a wide berth and constantly watched the front door, expecting Dora to knock on it at any moment. Liz hoped this new hyper-alertness would wear off. If not, she might have to think about moving into Gull Cottage so he could relax properly.

At that moment, it seemed a pretty good idea. She had taken up all the kitchen carpet in Kipper, but now the floor looked really horrible. The rubbing alcohol hadn't worked to shift the old glue, and it still remained in patches on the stone. She had to pick her way between the sticky bits so her slippers weren't pulled off her feet. Nelson wasn't too happy about it, either. He avoided the glue as much as he could, and the only place he deigned to sit was his basket. It hardly helped his current mood. Liz knew something that would cheer him up. She caught his eye.

'Walk?'

THEY WERE ABOUT HALFWAY up the abbey steps when Liz realised she'd made a mistake. She lowered herself onto a bench on one of the coffin steps and rubbed her aching knee.

'Sorry, Nelson,' she said. 'I don't think we're going to make it up there today.'

For once, he didn't seem too bothered. He sat sniffing the air, catching the scents of sand and sea, candy and seaweed, kippers and hotdogs, his nose twitching and ears lifting in the breeze. Liz took a deep breath and willed herself to wake up.

She looked up the steps, towards the abbey, and saw that someone was on their way down. At first, they were too far away to make out who it was, but it seemed to be someone bulky, with broad shoulders, carrying a bag. As the figure got closer, Liz realised it wasn't a big man at all, but a small young man with a huge rucksack, thumping down the steps in his boots.

'Morning, Niall,' she said when he had come into earshot. 'Lovely day.'

'If you say so.' He dropped his holdall and wrestled with his rucksack. It fell with a whump beside Nelson, making him flinch.

'Sorry, boy.' Niall ruffled the dog's ears by way of apology. 'Didn't mean to scare you.' He plonked himself on the bench beside Liz.

Liz took in his glum expression and the fact he seemed to be carrying all his worldly possessions.

'Is that you finished at the abbey, then?' she asked, trying to phrase it as tactfully as possible.

He nodded and wiped his nose with his sleeve. Liz thought he might be crying. She was careful not to look at him, but gazed out over the sea instead, giving him time to compose himself.

'She's fired me,' he said eventually. 'She says I lied about my degree, but I didn't. I *do* have a degree. Just not a 2:1 like I put on my CV.' He saw Liz looking at him. 'I got a third. Hardly a hanging offence.'

'No, it isn't.'

'She had it in for me. Because I know her secret.'

'What secret?'

'That she fancied the professor.'

'Really? I got the impression Dora didn't like him very much.'

'Oh, she liked him alright. More than that. *Much* more. I used to see her, when he wasn't looking, making puppy dog eyes at him.' He broke off and addressed Nelson. 'No offence, boy.' He turned back to Liz. 'The thing is, she *saw* me see. I guess my days were numbered.'

Liz realised he was probably right. Dora Spackle was a proud woman.

'What are you going to do now?' she asked.

He sighed, the weight of the world on his shoulders. 'Go back to Ireland, I suppose, but I barely have enough cash to get me there. And Ma can't really afford to keep me.'

'Why not stay here and get a job? One that pays? Then you can save up to go abroad.'

'Great idea. But I can't afford tourist prices. Even if I got a job, I'd be working hard just to pay for somewhere to stay.'

Liz was quiet, thinking. She hardly knew Niall, but had decided she liked him. Question was, did she like him enough to throw him a lifeline? She decided she did.

'Are you any good at DIY?'

'Eh?'

'Joinery. Tiling. Carpet fitting. That kind of thing.'

'Pretty decent. My da was a builder. Why?'

'I have somewhere you can stay. A cottage. But it needs doing up. You could find yourself a job and give me a hand in your spare time.'

'For real?' He grinned. 'That'd be grand!'

'It's no palace. You'd be roughing it.'

'As long as I have a sleeping bag and somewhere to put my head, I'll be fine.'

'One thing, though.' Liz looked at him, eyebrows raised. 'Gull Cottage is a *non-smoking* cottage.' She held his gaze for a beat.

He grinned and nodded. Message received.

NIALL DUMPED his rucksack and holdall in Gull, then came to Kipper for a cup of tea.

'Your name needs fixing,' he said.

'What?'

'Your cottage nameplate. By the front door.'

'Oh, yes. It's not the only thing.'

'So I see.' He eyed the kitchen floor. 'What's going on here?'

Liz poured hot water into two mugs.

'Bit of a disaster. The carpet was stuck down with glue.'

'A sandblaster will get that off, no problem,' he said. 'I can do it for you if you hire one.'

'Fantastic!' Liz grinned as she gave him his tea. Karma was already working in her favour.

'It will make a mess, though. When we blasted Aunt Berna's beams, her living room was like the Sahara for weeks.'

'Nothing that can't be cleaned.'

'For sure.' He took a sip. 'That's a grand cup of tea.'

Liz joined him at the table.

'I really appreciate you helping me out,' he said. 'You're a saint.'

'Hardly.'

His smile faded. 'I can't believe she fired me. Dora feckin' Spackle.'

Nelson growled. They both looked at him.

'What's up with him?' asked Niall.

'Dora feckin' Spackle,' said Liz.

Nelson growled again.

'Dora is Nelson's nemesis,' explained Liz, 'but I had no idea he knew her name.'

'Dora Spackle,' said Niall experimentally.

Nelson growled.

'Can't say I blame him,' said Niall. 'The woman's a nightmare. She really enjoyed putting the boot in this morning.'

'I *am* surprised about her and Professor Crowby,' said Liz. 'I had her tagged as a dyed-in-the-wool spinster.'

'It's never too late for love, Mrs Mac.' Niall's face was serene as he gulped the rest of his tea.

Liz looked at him thoughtfully. 'Maybe.'

'The prof was a weird choice, though, for sure, even for ...' He glanced at Nelson. 'She Who Shall Not Be Named.'

Liz smiled. 'Weird how?'

He shrugged. 'He could start a fight in an empty room. Always arguing with someone. The last time I saw him, he was having a row.'

'Oh?' Liz's interest was piqued. 'Who with?'

'That guy with the spooky shop on Baxtergate.'

'Wally Duguid?'

'Don't know his name. They were in the prof's car, in the museum car park.'

She remembered what Janet had said. 'They were friends, I think.'

'Didn't look like it to me. Looked like they were having a square go. Both of them red in the face and shouting.'

Interesting. 'You told the police, I suppose?'

He shrugged. 'They never asked me. They haven't asked me anything.'

'I don't suppose you could hear what they were shouting about?'

Niall shook his head. 'I kept my distance. "Hear no evil, see no evil" is my motto.'

'Very wise.' She wondered what had happened to "speak no evil" but then decided she didn't care. It wasn't a bad thing Niall was a gossip.

She saw he'd finished his tea. 'Right,' she said. 'We'd better get some stuff sorted out for you.'

She helped him carry a stack of supplies into Gull Cottage – towels, soap, crockery – then switched on the electricity and lit the boiler. She told him not to use the stove. It was easily as old as the one in Kipper Cottage and might not be safe. She promised to buy him an electric kettle, and left him standing in the kitchen, his belongings scattered over the swirly carpet. She realised, with some surprise, she'd felt a bit of a twinge as she left him there. She supposed it was her underdeveloped maternal instincts. She'd have to keep an eye on that – no one needed two mothers.

As soon as she got back to Kipper, she found her mobile phone.

12

'You were right,' said Kevin around a mouthful of sausage roll. 'The payments *were* from Wally Duguid.'

'All of them?'

Kevin nodded. 'Not from Chapel Antiques, but half a dozen other companies, all with Duguid registered as sole owner. The man's something of an entrepreneur.'

It was a few days later. Niall had settled in to Gull Cottage and had already managed to find himself a part-time job pulling pints in the Duke of York, the pub at the bottom of the abbey steps. Liz had booked a sandblaster for the coming weekend. She and Niall were now psyching themselves up for 'the Big Blast'. She'd started to clear the kitchen of furniture and had even persuaded Tilly and Mags to take Nelson in the café for the night. It had seemed the kindest thing to do, and she knew that Tilly and Mags would spoil him rotten.

While all this was going on, Kevin had been investigating Professor Crowby's links with Wally Duguid. Now, he and Liz were sitting in their usual shelter on the West Cliff, eating the packed lunch she'd brought them. The weather was overcast but mild. Seagulls swooped and wailed overhead.

'When did the payments start?' she asked. 'Was it after the girdle went missing?' She rubbed her still-aching knee.

Kevin swallowed his sausage roll and looked at her.

'Don't you remember last Thursday?' he asked.

She looked at him blankly.

'When I told you not to get involved?'

'Wasn't the information I gave you useful?'

'Yes, but ...'

'I'm not in any danger, am I?'

'No, but ...'

'And don't I make great sausage rolls?'

Kevin groaned. 'You're not taking this seriously, Liz. If Flint had any idea I was talking to you about the investigation, I could lose my job. I'm on a sticky wicket as it is.'

She felt a twinge of guilt.

'I'm sorry, Kevin. I am taking it seriously. Honestly. I'm not trying to poke my nose in; it's just I keep coming across information that might help you. The font. The theft of the girdle. Crowby's argument with Duguid. You wouldn't want me to keep it to myself, would you?'

'I suppose not.' He ran a hand through his hair, making it stick up like a schoolboy's. Liz resisted the urge to pat it back into place for him. Really, her maternal instincts were getting out of hand lately.

'I'm trying to help you keep your job,' she said, 'not lose it.'

He nodded. 'I know that. It's just ...' He tailed off and stared at the sea, as if debating something in his head. Then he seemed to come to a decision. 'I had a word with Duguid this morning.'

'Did you?' Liz sat forward on the bench. 'What did he say?'

'That he hardly knew Ian Crowby. He denies the argument in the car park ever happened. Says whoever saw it must have mistaken him for someone else.'

'And you believe that?'

'No. He was paying Crowby for something. And, having had a brief look at his finances, I'm pretty sure he's up to his armpits in all kinds of dodgy deals. The problem is proving it.'

'You think he has the girdle? Maybe he was paying Crowby in instalments for it?'

'Thirty payments of three hundred pounds?' Kevin's tone was doubtful. 'Even if he'd agreed to pay a quarter of what the girdle was worth ... twenty thousand ... it would still take an age to pay Crowby off.' He shook his head. 'It makes no sense.'

Liz had to agree. It hardly sounded like the work of a criminal mastermind.

'Does Flint know about Duguid? About his connections in the antique trade?'

'She doesn't think the girdle has anything to do with Crowby's murder. She says, and I quote: "People don't commit murder for a tatty bit of cloth." '

'Do you think she's right?'

'That it's a tatty piece of cloth?' He grinned. Liz was pleased he hadn't lost his sense of humour. 'I don't know about that. But I *do* know one thing – I'd love to take a proper look around Duguid's shop.'

'Can't you get a search warrant?'

Kevin rolled his eyes. 'You've been watching too much TV. You have no idea the hoops you have to jump through to get one. And even if I put the paperwork in, Flint would veto it. She wouldn't want to spend the money and man-hours on something she doesn't believe is connected to Crowby's death anyway.'

'So what's your next move?'

'Good old grunt work. Do some online sleuthing to see if I can spot the girdle for sale anywhere. Check the blood results from the font. Try to piece together Crowby's final hours in the town, and hope something meets in the middle.'

'Sounds like fun.'

'Yeah.' Kevin looked glum. He returned Liz's Tupperware. 'Thanks for lunch. The sausage rolls were great.'

'You're welcome.'

Iris Gladwell was in the Full Moon Café when Liz stopped by on her way home. Liz slid into the seat opposite, glad to get the weight off her leg. She'd found it hard to walk all the way from the West Cliff, and now her knee was *really* throbbing. She tried to ignore it.

'That looks nice,' she said, nodding at the remains of the old lady's cream tea. 'But I thought jam didn't agree with you?'

'IT DOESN'T, ON A FRIDAY. TODAY'S WEDNESDAY.'

'Oh.' Liz had no idea why that would make a difference, but decided not to ask.

'Did you get in touch with Janet Masters?' she asked instead.

'I DID,' boomed Iris. 'NICE LASS. SHAME ABOUT HER DAD.'

'Murder's a terrible thing.'

'I'M NOT TALKING ABOUT THAT. THE MAN WAS AN ARSE.'

'Oh.'

'A FIRST-CLASS ARSE.'

'You didn't say you knew him.'

Iris looked at her irritably.

'The other day,' prompted Liz, 'when we were talking

about the murder. You didn't say you knew him.'

'I DO CHANGEOVERS FOR COCKLESHELL COTTAGE IN WHITE HORSE YARD. I USED TO HEAR HIM. AND HER.' She sniffed. 'AT IT LIKE RABBITS.' She looked at her watch and pushed herself to her feet. 'ONLY AN HOUR BEFORE CHECK-IN AT THE CROW'S NEST.' She grabbed her bag. 'CATCH YOU LATER, LOVE.'

She was out of the door before Liz could say 'tell me more'. Liz thought about what she'd said. That fitted with the hairs she'd spotted in the hairbrush in Crowby's cottage. Long blonde hairs. Janet Masters might think her father was living alone there, but it seemed he had company. If he and his wife were talking about getting back together, might his lover have found out? Could it be a crime of passion?

'A one-woman whirlwind, that one.'

Liz turned to see Tilly carrying two mugs.

'I've never seen anyone eat a scone so fast.' She put the mugs on the table – tea for Liz and coffee for herself – and sat down with a groan of relief. 'How did Kevin like the sausage rolls?'

'Loved them.'

'My special recipe.'

'You won't tell him, will you?'

'As long as you make it worth my while.' It was Tilly who made the lunches Liz occasionally took to Kevin on the West Cliff. Liz would struggle to cobble together so much as a cheese sandwich from what she usually had in the fridge. She lived like a student, really, from one meal to the next. It hardly seemed worth planning ahead and shopping in advance just for herself. Bribing a police officer for information took much more culinary collateral than she was personally able to muster.

'What's new over there in Kevland?' asked Tilly. 'Anything interesting?'

'Wally Duguid was paying the professor for something in instalments.'

'The girdle?'

'It doesn't seem likely.'

'Well, whatever it was, I bet it's bent. He tried to fleece you for that bottle.'

'And you for the Hand of Glory.'

'Yeah, well ... I've been doing some research, and I think that price wasn't too far off the mark. They're not easy to come by.' Tilly took a sip of her coffee.

'I don't suppose you've heard anything more from DI Flint?' asked Liz.

'No, thank God. Poor old Kev, having her as his boss.'

'What kind of questions was she asking you?'

'Whether I'd ever been in the museum. What my favourite methods of breaking and entering used to be. Yada, yada, yada.'

'Did she ask you where you were on the night of the murder?'

Tilly shook her head.

'Kev says she doesn't think the theft and the murder are connected. But if so, why would she be interviewing you? She's serious crime.'

'How much was the girdle worth?'

'About eighty grand.'

'Well, that's pretty serious.'

'I suppose.' Liz took a gulp of tea.

'Wally Duguid would definitely want a slice of *that* action.'

'He would. He has to be mixed up in it somehow. Kevin wants to get a search warrant to take a look at his shop.'

'And?'

'He doesn't think he can.'

'Do you think the girdle is there?'

'Maybe.'

Tilly looked thoughtful. 'I'm not so sure Duguid would risk it.'

'Why?'

'He has no alarm system.'

'Really?' Liz was surprised.

'Not that I could see. No motion sensors. No window or door contacts. And his locks look like they were fitted by Mickey Mouse and Goofy.'

'You were busy while I was talking to him.'

'Old habits die hard.'

Their eyes met and held.

Mags appeared suddenly through the beaded curtain.

'Oh, hi, Liz. How's things?'

'Great, thanks.'

'Is Nelson ready for his play date here?'

'He is.' Liz grinned. 'The question is, are *you* ready?'

'Yes! We've cleared a nice cosy spot for his basket by the boiler and stocked up on doggy treats. We've even bought him a present.' Mags reached under the counter and brought out something pink and plastic. A pig. She squeaked it.

Liz laughed. 'He'll think he's died and gone to heaven.'

Mags pulled a face. 'Don't think I'm rude, but I have to go. I have to unpack the cash and carry.'

'I'll give you a hand in a minute,' said Tilly.

Mags disappeared again. Tilly stood up and stretched.

'Oooof.' Her joints cracked. 'I'm getting old.'

'Shut up!' Liz laughed. 'You're a spring chicken.'

'I don't get much exercise, stuck in here all day.' Tilly collected their mugs to take to the kitchen, without looking at Liz. 'I might go for a little walk later. Stretch my legs.'

Her tone was casual. Too casual. Liz frowned.

'I don't suppose you fancy a leg stretch, too?' Tilly's face was as mild as a Madonna's. 'About midnight?'

13

'You should get a doctor to look at that knee,' said Niall.

Liz knew he was right. As a nurse, she'd seen many elderly patients lose mobility unnecessarily because they hadn't addressed joint problems straightaway. But she didn't want to think of herself as 'elderly' just yet.

'I think it's getting better,' she said.

Niall snorted. 'My aunt Phil ignored a sore elbow once, and it swole to twice the size of a football.'

Liz stifled a grin. 'And what happened then?'

'It stiffened up, so she couldn't bend it anymore. She had to give up the shinty.'

'Oh no!' Liz couldn't hold back her smile any longer. Niall had an army of anecdotal aunts and uncles, each one a victim of undeserved misfortune.

'It's no laughing matter.' Niall feigned outrage. 'She played for Ireland. Had an international career.' But he couldn't quite hide his own smile. 'Call the doctor, will you?'

'Okay.' Liz threw up her hands in surrender. 'I'll do it tomorrow. See if they can fit me in.' In the few days that Niall

had been staying in Gull Cottage, it was hard to say who had
been mothering who.

'What time did you say your shift started?' asked Liz.

Niall looked at the clock. 'Feck!' He jumped up and
grabbed his coat. Even though he was supposed to be staying
in Gull, he spent more time in Kipper. Liz didn't mind at all.
She hadn't realised how lonely she had been, and suspected
he'd been lonely, too. Nelson escorted Niall to the door,
wagging his tail.

'What time will you finish?' she asked.

'Not 'til twelve. See you tomorrow.' He had to bang the
door twice on his way out to get it to shut properly.

LIZ LOOKED AT THE CLOCK. Eight o'clock. It was just as well
Niall was out of the way. She had things to do, and wanted no
awkward questions.

First things first. She dragged her toolbox out of the
cupboard under the stairs while Nelson watched from a safe
distance. He still didn't trust her not to lock him in there
again.

She rummaged in the wooden toolbox, which had been
her father's. It was huge, more of a chest than a box, with lift-
out trays and compartments for nails and screws. Liz always
struggled to find things in it. Tilly reckoned Wally Duguid's
doors were so flimsy they wouldn't need anything more
sophisticated than a crowbar to get in. Luckily, Liz had the
small one she used for levering off the cladding. She found it,
then chose a couple of screwdrivers to take as well, just in
case – one flat-head and one Phillips. She put them in her
backpack with the crowbar. She and Tilly had agreed that Liz
should carry the tools. It wouldn't go well for Tilly if, as a
convicted burglar, she was caught 'going equipped'.

Suddenly, the enormity of what she was doing hit Liz.

What the hell was she thinking? She closed the toolbox lid and sat on it. Why was she so invested in all this?

Well, first, and most importantly, she wanted to help Tilly. Inspector Flint had her in her sights, and Liz didn't like that one bit. By finding the real thief, they would clear Tilly's name. Even if the strategy of proving Tilly didn't commit one theft by helping her commit another didn't particularly stand up to scrutiny, Liz was prepared to do it if it got Tilly off the hook.

Second, she was curious about what Wally Duguid was up to. It was one thing to make a fair profit on the antiques he bought, but it was quite another to deliberately rip people off. He had offered her less than a quarter of what her sailing ship bottle was worth. And if he had tried to fleece her, he must be fleecing other people on a regular basis.

Third, she really, really wanted to know what had happened to Professor Crowby. Being the one who had found him on the clifftop, she felt she had a certain amount of 'skin in the game'. She was sure Crowby's death was connected with the girdle.

There was another reason, too. Maybe less obvious than the others, and certainly not as altruistic: she felt invested in something. Something important. She hadn't felt so alive since Mark's death.

She stood up. What should a burglar wear? Something dark, obviously. That could be a problem. She generally preferred light colours, but she might have something suitable tucked away with the clothes she kept for funerals.

It was dark when she woke up. Moonlight slanted through the roof window above her bed, dimmed every now and then by fast-moving clouds. For a moment she'd forgotten where she was, until St Mary's clock struck quarter to the hour, and she remembered her plans for the evening. She quickly swung her legs out of bed and dressed in the burglar outfit she'd laid out. She hadn't found anything suitable in her funeral wear, just skirts and tailored jackets that wouldn't give her much freedom of movement. Instead, she'd unearthed a pair of shiny black leggings and a dark grey fake-fur bolero she'd bought a decade before, on the off-chance she might have a party to go to at some point. She hadn't, but had never had the heart to throw them out, feeling it was a sad admission of an inadequate social life. They weren't really suitable for the activities of a lady thief and (she had to admit) were a bit age-inappropriate now, but at least they were better than a skirt suit, and were the best she could do under the circumstances. It was hard to get the leggings on over her knee. The nap she'd taken in preparation for her adventure hadn't dulled the ache or reduced the swelling. She took two painkillers and went downstairs.

The kitchen clock told her it was 11.52. She'd have to get a move on if she wasn't going to be late. She opened a can of dog food and gave it to Nelson, then made her escape while he had his head in his bowl. As she banged the door shut, she noticed the sign for Kipper Cottage was straight again. Niall must have fixed it. She made a mental note to thank him.

Henrietta Street was quiet. Even though there were quite a few pubs in the old town, most of the revellers tended to head in the other direction at closing time. But as she walked silently over the cobbles, she heard someone coming, whistling a tune – 'The Girl from Ipanema'. She ducked into a doorway just as Niall came into sight at the far end of the street. She held her breath. Luckily, he sauntered past her without turning his head. As soon as he'd gone, she hurried on her way.

Once again, she was beginning to question the wisdom of what she was about to do. The more she thought about it, the more she doubted Wally Duguid would actually have the girdle. And even if he did, he probably wouldn't be stupid enough to keep it in his antique shop. Yet ... yet they might find something linking him to the theft, or even to the murder. She made up her mind to 'screw her courage to the sticking place'. As she approached the café, a shadow detached itself from the doorway. Tilly, dressed in a black hoodie and joggers, looked her over and gave a low wolf whistle.

'Well, hello, party animal.'

'Shut up. It was all I could find that was dark.'

'I hope we don't come across someone looking for a good time. He'll certainly think you're up for it.'

They made their way to the new town, over the swing bridge. There were a few people about, mainly groups of young people heading home, but no one paid them any attention. As they turned into Baxtergate, Liz realised her heart was thumping, and made a conscious effort to steady her breathing. About twenty yards down the street, Tilly ducked into an alleyway that ran between two of the shops. Liz was surprised. For some reason, she'd imagined them breaking into the front of the chapel, but now she realised that would be stupid. It would be horribly exposed and might even be in view of CCTV cameras in the street. She followed Tilly down the alley, which smelled of pee, and into a narrow lane that ran behind the shops. She had had no idea it even existed. Clearly, she was in the hands of a professional.

The alleyway didn't have street lamps, but it was still light enough to see, thanks to the moon that came and went behind the clouds. The back of the chapel was easy to spot, jutting above the other shops. It was protected by a high wall with a gate. Liz took off her rucksack, intending to give Tilly the crowbar, but Tilly pushed at the gate instead. It just swung open. Tilly grinned.

'You'd be surprised how often that happens,' she whispered. 'It's always worth a try.'

The chapel yard was small and stacked with stuff – old statuary, chimney pots and broken furniture. Liz felt safer there than in the alley, less exposed, even though she was now technically on someone else's property without permission. Tilly scanned the windows with a professional eye, then the door. She turned the handle ... and the door opened. They looked at each other in surprise.

'Like I said, always worth a try.'

'Perhaps we should call the police?' suggested Liz.

'Eh?'

'In case someone's broken in?'

'Seriously?'

Liz supposed it was a daft thing to say, but she was still uneasy. 'What if there's someone already in there?'

'There isn't. There's no lights on. He just forgot to lock the door, that's all. Come on.'

Tilly went in. Liz hesitated, then followed.

It was darker in the shop than it had been in the yard, but they could see they were in a kitchen. There was a butler's sink, an electric kettle and a small fridge. Like the yard, it was stacked with old stuff in various states of disrepair.

'This way,' hissed Tilly.

As she was following Tilly out the door, Liz stifled a shriek. Something was staring at her! It took a moment for her to realise it was a taxidermy head. The badger glared beadily back at her as she tried to get her hammering heart under control.

It was so dark in the corridor that Liz had to feel her way along the wall.

'I can't see,' she hissed. 'Can't we use a torch?'

'Too risky,' Tilly hissed back. 'Don't be such a wuss.'

They passed a door Liz recognised, with 'Laundry' etched on the glass.

'This is it! The office.'

Tilly retraced her steps, and they went in together. It was pitch-black inside. Liz remembered there had only been one tiny window in it, and that it had been crowded with furniture. No sooner had the memory come to her than she tripped over something and whacked her leg. The pain in her knee, previously dulled by painkillers, came crashing back.

'Ooof!' she gasped. 'This is impossible. We can't find anything if we can't see.'

'Hang on a minute. Don't move.'

She heard Tilly fumble for her phone, and after a second, light flashed into Liz's face. She shielded her eyes.

'Are you okay?' asked Tilly, face ghostly behind her phone.

'I tripped on something.'

Tilly shone the light down. And froze.

Wally Duguid lay on his back, staring glassily at the ceiling. His mouth was open and crammed with something dark that spilled out, over his chest and on to the floor. At first, Liz thought it was fabric of some kind, but as she looked closer, she saw it wasn't.

It was copper coins.

14

'So ... let's go over this again,' said Inspector Flint. 'You and your friend Matilda Fairweather were "taking a stroll", after midnight, down the alley that runs behind Walter Duguid's shop – an alley that leads precisely nowhere. You heard a noise in the shop, on the other side of the yard and through the back door, that made you go and investigate rather than call the police.'

'That's it exactly,' said Liz. 'We heard a crash.'

Flint narrowed her eyes. 'Matilda Fairweather says you heard a scream.'

Trust Tilly to get creative.

'It was a crash and a scream.'

Flint glanced at Constable Williams, who was sitting beside her. He looked weary. It was three o'clock in the morning, and DI Flint had been questioning Liz for forty-five minutes after keeping her waiting on her own for hours. Flint had clearly already questioned Tilly. Liz wondered whether Kevin was in the station. If so, he was giving them a wide berth. Probably wise.

'A crash *and* a scream.' Flint tapped her fingers on the table. 'Okay. Let's pretend for a minute that's true, and talk about the contents of your rucksack.'

'Is it possible to get some painkillers from somewhere? My knee's really hurting.'

'Is there any particular reason you were carrying a crowbar?'

'I just forgot to take it out. I've been doing a lot of DIY.'

'With a crowbar?'

'Mm. I've been taking cladding off the wall.'

'And you normally keep the crowbar in your rucksack?'

'Yes. It's sort of a tool bag cum rucksack. I sometimes forget to take the tools out. There are probably other tools in there, too.' She maintained her look of innocence.

'You carry them around town with you?' Flint's expression clearly said she didn't believe it. 'When you're "taking a stroll", when you're shopping?'

'Sometimes, if I've forgotten to take them out.' The way Flint kept saying "taking a stroll" was beginning to irritate Liz. 'We didn't break into the shop. The door was open. And the gate.'

'That's true, ma'am,' said Constable Williams. 'There were no signs of a forced entry.'

'When I want your input, Williams, I'll ask for it.'

His long face grew even longer.

Liz stifled a yawn.

'Are we keeping you up, Mrs McLuckie?' Flint was finding it harder and harder to hide her frustration.

'Not at all.' Liz was trying her best not to antagonize her.

'Homicide is a serious business. As one of the people who found Mr Duguid, you're key to our enquiries.'

'Of course.'

'You seem to be making a habit of finding dead bodies.'

Liz resisted the urge to say she was just lucky that way.

Finding Wally Duguid dead in such horrible circumstances had shocked her to the core. Now the adrenalin was wearing off, she was feeling a little shaky, and the pain in her knee was also making it hard to think. Flint glared and tapped her fingers on the table. The silence stretched.

'Where were you and Miss Fairweather going?'

'Nowhere in particular. Like I said, we were just taking a stroll.'

Flint looked at Liz's leggings and bolero. 'You're not dressed for a stroll.'

'I'm not dressed for a burglary, either.'

Flint nodded, acknowledging the point. 'Why "stroll" down that particular alley? Why not "stroll" on the beach or the clifftop or the pier?'

Liz hid her annoyance. If Flint said "stroll" one more time, she was going to explode. She shrugged instead. 'We were curious. We'd never been down that alley before.'

'Why didn't you call the police when you heard the noise in the shop – whatever it was.'

'I don't know. I suppose we were worried someone had hurt themselves.'

Flint harrumphed.

'I really would appreciate a painkiller, Inspector, if you have one.'

A look of intense irritation crossed Flint's face. She nodded at Williams, who got up and went out of the interview room, leaving the door ajar.

Flint leaned across the table. 'Let's stop all this.'

'Sorry?'

'Why not save us all the time and trouble and tell me what's really going on?'

'I don't know what you mean.' To Liz's relief, they were interrupted by a knock on the door. Kevin pushed it open. He didn't look at Liz.

'Inspector?'

'What is it?'

'The preliminary medical examination. It looks as if Duguid died early evening, around seven pm.'

Flint glared at him. 'Why don't you just use a megaphone, Ossett, so *everyone* can hear?'

'Sorry, ma'am. I thought you should know.' Now he did look at Liz, his expression carefully neutral. 'Mrs McLuckie and Miss Fairweather couldn't have had anything to do with his death.'

'Bloody hell!' Flint couldn't contain her frustration any longer. 'That's for *me* to decide, not you.' She glared at Liz. 'Or anyone else.'

Kevin ducked out again just as Williams reappeared carrying a glass of water and a packet of painkillers. He gave them to Liz and sat down.

'Mrs Duguid's here,' he said to Flint. 'She says Mrs McLuckie and Miss Fairweather were in the shop last week.'

'Really?' Flint's eyes drilled into Liz.

Liz took two of the tablets.

'I had a couple of things I wanted him to look at,' she said.

'Such as?'

'Ginger beer bottles.'

'Beer bottles?'

'Mm. One is quite rare, apparently.' She decided not to say anything about the fact that Duguid had tried to rip her off. Knowing Flint, she'd probably think it was motive for a revenge attack. Maybe not murder – it looked like they were off the hook for that – but definitely burglary. Liz met Flint's gaze and held it.

'Okay, we're done here.' Flint stood up and straightened her skirt. 'I find it hard to believe your involvement is coinci-dental. If I get even so much as a sniff you're trying to interfere in this investigation – in either of them – I'll have you back in here so fast your feet won't touch the floor.'

Liz nodded and headed gratefully for the door.

'Mrs McLuckie?'

Liz turned.

'For future reference, dead men don't scream.'

Liz met Tilly at the duty sergeant's counter, retrieving her things. The crowbar and screwdrivers clanked as the sergeant handed her own rucksack back to her. Once they had signed for everything, they retreated to a safe distance.

'Have you seen Kevin at all?' whispered Tilly.

'Briefly,' said Liz. 'You?'

Tilly shook her head.

Liz took Tilly by the elbow. 'Let's get out of here.'

It was almost dawn outside, with light just starting to pearl the sky in the east. The liquid notes of a blackbird trickled into the air. Kevin was waiting for them, leaning against his car with his arms folded. He looked from one to the other, inscrutable, waiting for one of them to speak.

'Sorry,' said Liz after a few beats of silence.

Kevin said nothing.

'We were just ...' Tilly began.

'You know what?' interrupted Kevin. 'I don't want to hear it.' Two spots of colour glowed in his cheeks. 'I told you – specifically told you – not to get involved. And when I mentioned not being able to get a search warrant for the shop, Liz, I didn't expect the both of you to just march in there.' He glared at Tilly. 'Don't you care if you go back to prison?'

'Of course I do, but ...'

Kevin held up his hand. 'Just ... don't.'

Liz realised how very angry he was.

'We really are sorry, Kevin.'

He shook his head. Tilly made a move for the passenger door of the car, but Kevin blocked her.

'I'm not taking you home,' he said. 'You can walk.'

'We'll see you tomorrow night, though?' pleaded Tilly. 'For mah-jong?'

He didn't answer, just shook his head as if he couldn't believe what he was hearing, and headed back into the station. Liz and Tilly watched him go. They walked back to the old town in silence.

The town centre was pretty much deserted apart from Mike the fishmonger in his van, who stopped for them at the pedestrian crossing beside the station. He waved to Liz and drove on, on his way to the fish quay for the morning catch.

As they approached the café, Tilly turned to Liz.

'Do you think he'll ever forgive us?' she asked.

'Mmm?' Liz was distracted. There was something niggling at the back of her brain, but she couldn't put her finger on it.

'Kevin,' prompted Tilly. 'I've never seen him so mad.'

'I don't know. I hope so.'

'It's been quite a night, hasn't it?'

Liz nodded. 'Poor old Wally Duguid.'

'Why do you think he did that?' asked Tilly. 'The killer? Why did he stuff his mouth with one- and two-pence pieces?'

'I don't know.' Liz had been wondering the same thing. 'It smacks a bit of Old Testament retribution, doesn't it? Filthy lucre?'

'He certainly liked money. Perhaps he ripped the killer off?'

'Perhaps.' Whatever the killer's motivation, Liz guessed she would dream about finding Wally Duguid's body for quite some time to come.

After Tilly had let herself into the side door of the café, Liz lingered. She wanted to go home and get some sleep, but there was something bothering her. Something her exhausted brain was trying to process. Was it something she'd heard? Something she'd seen?

It came to her in a flash. She turned around and headed back the way she'd come.

15

W hitby Fish Market was a low, red-roofed building, with a small central brick section flanked by two long white sheds, punctuated with porthole windows and numbered hatches. Pier Road ran along one side, and it was open to the harbour on the other so that trawlers and other fishing boats could unload their catch straight into the market hall. Liz had only ever seen it during the day, when it was silent and shuttered.

It looked very different now.

All the doors and hatches were open, spilling light and noise onto the quayside. There were a dozen or so vans of various sizes pulled up outside. She spotted Mike's van among them, with its back doors open, but there was no sign of the fishmonger himself.

She hesitated at one of the open doors into the market, unsure whether, as a civilian, she was actually allowed inside. It looked quite daunting: a cavernous space lit by fluorescent strip lights, bustling with life. There didn't seem to be any kind of door person, so she went in.

All her senses reeled at the assault. The first and most

noticeable thing was the noise. The big space echoed with the sound of people shouting to each other, the clash and rattle of metal trolleys, and phones ringing. The air was cold. There was a smell too. Not of fish – the new catch was too fresh for that – but of brine and the darker aroma of blood.

She wandered, wide-eyed, around the hall, being careful not to slip on the wet floor. Everywhere she looked there were wooden pallets piled with polystyrene boxes and plastic crates, filled with ice and fish of all kinds: massive codling, smaller herrings, glossy striped mackerel, sea bream, sea bass, and eels. Some were bagged and boxed; some displayed in ice with prices. There was shellfish, too: small nets of cockles and mussels, slippery grey prawns piled on trays waiting to be scooped into bags, and crates of crabs and lobster, claws waving like pugilists.

Most of the fish traders were dressed in hoodies and sweats, some with aprons, some in rubber boots. Quite a few of the older men wore white coats and flat caps. They tapped on cash registers, heaved boxes onto weighing scales and shouted into mobile phones. Their customers were mostly wholesale buyers, Liz guessed, although there were also a few more ordinary-looking people wandering up and down with carrier bags – the owners and chefs of some of the smaller restaurants, perhaps, and maybe a few civilians who preferred to buy their fish fresh. Liz liked fresh fish, too, but didn't think it worth getting up at four o'clock in the morning for it.

Suddenly remembering what she was there for, she stopped an official-looking man with a high-viz vest and earpiece.

'I'M LOOKING FOR MIKE HOWSON?' She had to shout to be heard.

The man didn't answer her, but pointed to the far end of the hall. She made her way there and saw a youngster with a beanie hat and rubber gloves, shovelling prawns into plastic bags. She caught his eye.

'MIKE HOWSON?'

'MIKE!' bellowed the lad. 'LADY HERE FOR YOU!'

A familiar red-cheeked figure peered round a stack of pallets. He looked astonished.

'Mrs McLuckie? What are you doing here?'

'Can we have a chat?'

'Pardon?'

'CAN WE TALK OUTSIDE?'

He nodded and held up his index finger. 'Give me one minute. I'm nearly done here.'

She watched him finish stacking his trolley with polystyrene boxes, then followed as he trundled it outside onto the quayside. They stopped at the open doors of his van.

'What is it I can do for you?' He wiped his hands on a cloth he had in the back.

'This might seem like a strange question, but did you see Professor Crowby the morning he was killed?'

Mike's red face grew solemn. 'As it happens, I did. Reckon I was probably one of the last people ever to talk to him. A spooky feeling, that.'

'It must be.'

'I'd just dropped off a delivery to one of the fish restaurants in the market square, when I saw the prof heading towards me. I was a bit surprised, if I'm honest. I don't normally see people up and about that time of the day ... except for you and Nelson, of course.'

'I don't suppose you sold him a fish, did you?'

'No.' Mike shook his head. 'I gave him one. A nice little herring for his breakfast. I know he likes herring, you see. He often used to buy it in my shop. I didn't have a carrier bag or anything with me, so we wrapped it up in some paper he had in his pocket.'

Liz could imagine what had happened: Ian Crowby in a hurry, Mike making him take a fish he probably didn't want, and then, to crown it all, having to wrap it in something he had in his pocket.

Mike sighed. 'I don't suppose he ever got to eat that little fish, did he? What a waste.'

Liz wasn't sure if he meant Crowby's life or the herring. Kevin hadn't mentioned the fish was wrapped in paper, and Liz was pretty sure he would've done if it had been when the body was examined. So what had happened to it?

'Do you remember what kind of paper it was?' she asked.

'Well, now, that's a question.' He scratched his head. 'I don't rightly recall. It was quite a big bit, maybe A4, I reckon. Had writing on it. Could have been a list of some kind?'

'Mm.'

Mike peered at her anxiously. 'Is that any help at all?'

Liz wasn't sure if it was, but smiled at the fishmonger anyway. 'Yes, thanks. I'll let you get on.'

'Much obliged.' He closed the van doors. 'Give my love to Nelson.'

16

'You look awful,' said Niall. 'Did your knee keep you awake last night?' He smeared marmalade on his toast and took a bite.

Liz briefly considered telling him about her nocturnal adventures, but decided against it. He'd find out soon enough. The whole town would once the Whitby grapevine got going. He took her silence as confirmation.

'Perhaps we should postpone the Big Blast on Saturday?'

Liz looked around her almost-empty kitchen. They'd moved everything out ahead of sandblasting the floor, and taped all the electrical sockets so they wouldn't get sand in them. They'd also put plastic sheeting over the windows so they wouldn't get scratched. After all that prep work, she didn't want to postpone if she could help it. She shook her head.

'I'll see if I can get an appointment at the doctor's today.'

'You said that yesterday.'

'I will. I promise.'

Niall finished his toast. 'I'll take Nelson out if you can't manage. I know he likes it up at the abbey. Don't you, boy?'

Nelson wagged his tail. He had no idea what Niall was saying, but clearly knew he was being spoken to. He couldn't believe his good luck when Niall stood up and took his lead off the hook. Niall avoided the bouncing dog, spotted Liz's phone on the kitchen counter, picked it up and handed it to her.

'Doctor,' he said. 'Now.'

SHE WASN'T able to get an appointment until four o'clock that afternoon, so she spent the day in her sitting room, reading. She told herself she was taking it easy because of her knee, but knew, deep down, she wasn't going out because she wanted to avoid gossip. It would be a miracle if people hadn't heard she'd found Wally Duguid dead in his shop and had been taken to the police station.

She thought about what Mike had told her at the fish market. The fish in Crowby's pocket had been wrapped in paper, paper that hadn't been there when the police examined his body. Had the killer taken it? If so, why? Was it a list? What kind of list would Ian Crowby be carrying around in his pocket?

At about two o'clock, there was a knock at the door. Nelson jumped up and clattered down the stairs, barking. Liz put down her book and her mug of tea and peered out the window. All she could see was the top of a dark head. She thought it might be Mags, but wasn't sure. Whoever it was knocked again. Nelson barked again. Liz realised she had to answer it.

It was Mags.

'Can I come in?' she asked, face serious.

'Of course.' Liz showed her into the kitchen. 'I'm sorry, there's nowhere to sit down here at the moment. I'll put the kettle on, and we can go upstairs, if you—'

'No, it's okay.' Mags cut her off. 'I'm not staying long.' She looked awkward. There was obviously something she wanted to say, but didn't know how.

'How's Tilly?' asked Liz.

'She's fine. You know what she's like. Everything's a big adventure.' Mags took a deep breath. 'I want to ask you a favour. If she suggests getting involved in anything like this again, please try to talk her out of it.'

Liz felt a lurch of guilt. It was debatable who should have talked who out of their trip to Chapel Antiques.

Mags continued. 'We've worked really hard for what we have now ... for the café ... for each other. I don't want her to risk it all for some silly ... I'm not sure what it was, exactly.'

'Me neither. I'm sorry,' said Liz. 'It was my fault. My suggestion.' That wasn't strictly true, but she felt Mags needed to hear it. 'I should have had more sense than to get her involved. It won't happen again. Not with me, anyway. I promise.'

Mags nodded, satisfied.

'Are you sure you don't want a cup of tea? The kettle's only just boiled.'

Mags shook her head. 'I've got to get back to the café. I only popped out for a few minutes, and Tilly's on her own. We really do have to get some extra help.' She patted Nelson, then headed back to the door.

As she stepped outside, she looked again at Liz. 'Thanks,' she said. She hesitated. 'Tilly ... well, she's Tilly. She can be a handful at times, but I love her.'

'I do, too.'

Mags nodded, smiled, and left. When Liz had closed the door behind her, she leaned against it. She felt bad, leading Tilly astray when she had so much at stake. She'd forgotten that not everyone had as little to lose as she did. There was no one she was accountable to.

The thought brought tears to her eyes. What would Mark have made of her escapade? She had no idea. All she knew was she'd have given anything just to feel his arms around her, to hear him laugh at her and tell her everything was going to be alright. She still missed him, very much, even after five years. Perhaps she did need grief counselling after all?

When it was time for her doctor's appointment, she took a taxi there. Dr Prakash, a comfortable-looking woman in her mid-forties, prodded and poked at her knee and made her bend and straighten it a few times before delivering her verdict.

'You've damaged the anterior cruciate ligament. Twisted it, I think, rather than torn it, which is good news. Tennis, was it?'

'Ripping up carpet.'

The doctor laughed. 'I'll strap it for you, but you do need to keep it moving. Really, you need to see a physiotherapist. I'll refer you to an NHS one, but it could take weeks to come through. In the meantime, if you can afford it, you'd be better off going private. There's a physiotherapist in the town I can recommend.' She took a business card from her desk and gave it to Liz.

'Thank you,' said Liz. 'I'll think about it.'

SHE TOOK a taxi to Benedict's that evening. She thought briefly about crying off because of her knee, but knew that would be cowardice. She had to face Kevin at some point, and should probably just get it over with. No doubt Benedict would also have something to say about their criminal enterprise. She was unaccountably nervous about that.

When the taxi dropped her off, she saw Tilly coming up the street, and waited at the gate for her to catch up.

'How are you?' asked Liz.

'I've been better,' said Tilly. 'Mags hasn't spoken to me all day. Can't say I blame her.'

Clearly, Mags hadn't told her about her visit to Kipper Cottage. Liz thought she probably shouldn't mention it either.

'We were a bit daft, weren't we?' she said instead.

'One way of putting it.' Tilly gave a wry grin. 'I'd do it again, though.'

'You would?'

'Hell yeah! Wouldn't you?' Tilly opened the gate. 'I've never seen a dead body before. Not just dead, but murdered. What a rush!'

Liz gave her what she hoped was a quelling look as they rang the bell. Tilly tried to compose her expression into one of contrition. The door opened. Benedict glared at them from the doorstep.

'I don't know if I should let you in,' he muttered. 'Are my valuables safe?'

Liz and Tilly stared at him for a beat, dismayed; then his face broke into a grin. 'Come in, for heaven's sake.'

'Is Kevin here?'

'Not yet,' said Benedict. 'We can enjoy the calm before the storm.'

They followed him through to the kitchen. Liz felt herself relaxing. It wasn't just the warmth and welcoming atmosphere of the kitchen, but the realisation that Benedict wasn't going to be judgemental about their adventures. She hadn't known it was so important to her. They gave him a quick summary of what had happened, with Tilly elaborating on certain points for dramatic effect.

'He was stone dead. There were coins in his mouth, on his chest and all over the floor. It was totally horrific,' she said cheerfully.

'I can see how badly it's affected you,' said Benedict, ironic. 'What about you, Liz?'

His eyes found hers. Liz felt tears prickle her eyes again. Really, she was being ridiculous. She stroked the cat on her knee to cover it.

'I'm fine.'

His eyes lingered. 'Really?'

'Really. I just feel bad for putting Kevin on the spot.'

'Ah ... yes. He called this afternoon. His boss has finally found out he knows you both. She's not happy.'

'Blood and thunder,' said Tilly. 'Poor Kev.'

They heard the front door open and close.

'Talk of the devil,' muttered Tilly. 'Here we go.'

Liz braced herself. They heard Kevin take his coat off. It seemed an age before he came into the kitchen, and Liz wondered what he was doing. She wished he would just get on with it. He came into the kitchen carrying a large paper bag, which he put on the kitchen counter before turning to face them.

Liz took a deep breath.

'Kevin,' she began, 'I can't begin to tell you how sorry ...'

He held up his hand. He looked serious, but not angry. Liz was relieved. She'd been a little shocked by the red-cheeked, tight-lipped detective he'd been the night before.

'Before you say anything,' he said. 'I have something for both of you.'

Tilly and Liz exchanged a nervous look. What could it be? Liz lifted the cat off her lap. Kevin rummaged in the bag and brought out two parcels carefully wrapped in brown paper. He gave one to each of them. Liz caught Benedict's eye and lifted an eyebrow. He shook his head. No idea.

'You go first,' said Tilly to Liz.

'No.' Kevin sat down. 'Both together.'

They opened the parcels and took out the contents. Two striped tee-shirts and black eye masks.

'For the next time you go for a "stroll",' said Kevin. 'That outfit of yours, Liz.' He shook his head at the memory. 'I thought you'd been brought in for soliciting.'

Liz gasped with shock at the insult, then felt laughter bubble. Kevin grinned.

'What the hell?' spluttered Tilly. 'I thought you were furious.'

'I am. Or rather, I was. Until Flint got hold of me this afternoon. She wanted to know why I hadn't told her I knew you both. Which I *had*. She just hadn't listened. Then she shouted at me for twenty minutes in front of everyone about "consorting with undesirables". Let's just say it made me realise where my loyalties lie.'

Tilly put on her mask.

'How do I look?' she asked.

'Undesirable,' said Liz. 'Very, very undesirable.'

They all burst out laughing.

'Seriously, though,' said Kevin when everyone had got their breath back, 'I realised just how much Flint has it in for me. My days in the force really are numbered unless I can catch this killer.' He looked at Liz and Tilly. 'I know I'll be wasting my breath telling you not to get involved, so I reckon I have a better chance with your help. As long as you promise me one thing.'

'What?' asked Liz.

'Please, please don't be brought in for questioning again. I don't think my nerves can take it.'

'We'll do our best,' said Liz.

Kevin nodded. 'I don't know about you, but I could do with a drink.'

Benedict stood. 'There's wine in the fridge, and I made samosas.'

In the conservatory, Liz noticed the table hadn't been set for mah-jong. Benedict had guessed they wouldn't get to it. They poured the wine and settled themselves comfortably.

'So,' said Tilly, brandishing an Indian pastry at Kevin, 'if we're going to be your deputies, you'd better fill us in on what's happening.'

'Not much as far as Duguid's concerned. We're still processing the scene. But it looks like he let his killer in.'

'He knew him?' asked Benedict.

'Probably. There was no sign of a break-in or even much of a struggle.'

'What about cause of death?' asked Liz.

'Early to say, but probably strangulation. The coins happened post-mortem.'

'You're sure the two deaths are linked?' asked Benedict.

Kevin raised his eyebrows. 'We haven't had a murder in Whitby for years, and then we get two at once? Victims who knew each other? It's too much of a coincidence for them not to be connected.'

'What about Crowby?' asked Liz. 'Any progress there?' She briefly thought about mentioning the fish, but decided not to. It wasn't much of a lead.

'The water in the font is definitely the same as the water in Crowby's lungs,' said Kevin. 'And there was epithelial tissue on the stone that matched his DNA. But the blood you found wasn't his.'

'The killer cut himself on the window when he broke into the church,' said Liz. 'I saw the window. It couldn't have been easy.'

'Maybe.' Kevin nodded.

'Were there any fingerprints?' asked Tilly.

'Not that we could find. The killer either wore gloves or wiped everything down afterwards.'

'I'm betting gloves,' said Tilly. 'It's just too much of a pain to wipe stuff down. But if he was wearing gloves, surely he wouldn't have cut himself?'

'Glass can cut through leather,' said Liz.

'I suppose,' agreed Tilly.

'Whoever it was,' said Benedict, 'they must be strong. Crowby was a tall man. It must have taken a lot of effort to drag him up to the basin and hold him there while he drowned.'

'Unless there were two of them,' chipped in Liz.

Kevin looked dismayed. 'I hadn't thought of that.'

Liz took pity. 'But it's probably just one person. Which must be a man. That eliminates Crowby's girlfriend, at least.'

'Girlfriend?' said Kevin. "I thought he was separated from his wife? I thought he lived alone?'

'So did I. Until I saw a hairbrush in his cottage. Either he has a very shaggy golden retriever or a girlfriend with long blonde hair.'

Kevin scratched his head. 'I wonder who it is.'

'That's no mystery,' said Benedict.

Everyone looked at him.

'It's Whitby's worst-kept secret. Ian Crowby was having an affair with Myrtle Duguid.'

They all stared at him in astonishment.

'I thought everyone knew,' he said. 'They were hardly discreet about it.'

' "At it like rabbits",' murmured Liz.

'Eh?' Tilly gave her a quizzical look.

Kevin was glaring at Benedict. 'Why didn't you tell me? Didn't you think it might help the investigation? Either of them?'

'This is Yorkshire, not Hollywood. People don't go round killing each other in fits of passion. And, by all accounts, Wally was glad to have Myrtle occupied.'

'He *knew*?' asked Kevin.

'Everyone knew. I thought *you* did. That's why I didn't mention it to you.'

Kevin rolled his eyes. 'This bloody town.'

Liz was silent. Benedict caught her eye.

'Penny for them?' he said.

'I'm not sure they're worth that much,' she said. 'But you have to wonder, don't you? Maybe we've been barking up the wrong tree. Maybe the murders have nothing to do with the girdle at all.'

17

The Big Blast went ahead as planned, at ten o'clock on Saturday morning. Thanks to Dr Prakash's expert strapping, Liz was able to carry out her part of the mission without too much trouble. She dropped Nelson early at the café, then picked up a rented van before collecting the blaster, compressor and protective clothing from the tool hire shop. Back at Kipper, she helped Niall into the overalls and protective hood. She had to stifle her laughter – he looked like a skinny orange stormtrooper.

'Right,' he said, voice muffled behind the visor. 'You'd better make yourself scarce, Mrs Mac. This is going to get messy.'

She retreated to the van in the street and started the compressor. For the next two hours, she sat in the van, watching sand and dust billow from the open door of the cottage, apologising to passers-by and dreading the mess she knew she was going to have to clean up afterwards. Eventually, an orange figure appeared through the dust in the doorway and gave her the thumbs-up. She turned off the compressor. Niall stepped out of the cottage and closed the door behind him. He took off the visor and hood and ran a glove through his sweat-soaked hair.

'I wouldn't go in there for a few hours,' he said. 'Silicosis isn't a pretty way to go, as my uncle Cillian would tell you. If he was still alive.'

Liz knew better than to ask for details. 'What about the glue?' she asked instead, handing him a can of Coke.

'It came off grand.' He gulped the drink. 'It's as clean as a nun's—'

'Fantastic,' interrupted Liz. 'You'd better get out of these things. I'll take everything back to the hire shop while you have a shower. Then I'll buy you lunch.'

It always astonished Liz how much food Niall could tuck into his skinny frame. She watched him polish off a full English breakfast, several slices of bread and butter, a scone and four mugs of tea before he leaned back and patted his stomach.

'Ooof,' he groaned. 'I needed that.'

'Clearly.' Liz caught Tilly's eye over the counter and winked. Nelson had been sitting at Niall's feet throughout his feast, gazing up at him, even though Liz had a strict 'no feeding from the table' rule. She guessed Niall had been sneaking him food in Kipper Cottage when she wasn't looking. Nelson was definitely looking thicker around the middle – although, to be fair, that probably had as much to do with the fact she hadn't been able to walk him properly because of her knee.

'More tea, Niall?'

'Please.'

Tilly topped up his mug from her big teapot. Realising there was no further prospect of food, Nelson picked up his plastic pig and took it behind the counter. Every now and then, they heard it squeak.

'Is it okay if I come to get him about six?' Liz asked Tilly.

'You can leave him here all night if you like. Mags adores him.'

'Perhaps you should get a dog?' suggested Liz.

Tilly laughed. 'We have enough on our plate, thank you very much.'

'I think a dog's a grand idea.' Niall smirked. 'Good as a deterrent.'

Tilly narrowed her eyes. 'A deterrent to?'

'Burglars.' Niall snorted with laughter.

Tilly raised her hand as if she was going to swipe him around the ear. Just then, Liz spotted a familiar figure passing the window. She jumped up.

'Excuse me.'

Outside on the street, Benedict was headed somewhere in a hurry. Liz had to call his name twice before he stopped and she could catch up with him.

'Hello!' he said. 'I thought you were doing the Big Blast today?'

'It's done. It went well, I think, although I haven't seen the results yet.' She hesitated. 'I wanted to ask if you're going to your grief support group tonight?'

He looked surprised. 'I am.'

'Can I come with you?'

'Of course.' His smile was warm. 'That'd be lovely.'

LOVELY WASN'T a word Liz would have used to describe the venue she found herself in six hours later. The Eskmouth Community Hall was a bare space with a splintery wooden floor, used for local groups like the Sea Scouts and the Amateur

Dramatic Society. It smelled of dust and stale sweat, reminding Liz of her old school gymnasium and embarrassing hours spent on unfathomable apparatus. Not a particularly nice memory. There were more people there than she thought there would be, about a dozen in total, mostly older folk, but also a few younger faces. Some she recognised. She nodded to Ryan Goddard as they gathered with the others around the tea urn.

'How are you, Ryan?' She was quite surprised to see him there. She didn't have him down as much of a talker anyway, much less someone who would unburden himself to strangers.

'Not too bad, thanks,' he said. He took his tea to one of the plastic seats. She was right. Not much of a talker. But she supposed just being there with other grieving people could be therapeutic. She sipped her own tea gratefully. She'd spent the afternoon dusting and sweeping, and even though she'd worn a face mask and had taken a shower afterwards, her mouth and eyes still felt gritty.

As she sipped, she watched Benedict across the room, talking to Reverend Garraway. Benedict had warned Liz she'd have to make her own way home, as he and the Reverend had a squash court booked at the sports centre afterward. They clearly got on well. Liz felt a twinge of ... what? Jealousy? Ridiculous. She went to sit down, annoyed at herself. She sat between an older gent and a younger woman, who both smiled and nodded. The Reverend took her own seat in the circle, beside Benedict.

'Hello again, everyone. I see a couple of new faces this week. Welcome. Let me just explain a little bit about our group. This isn't a therapy session. I'm not a trained thera-pist, and no one is going to compel anybody to talk if they don't feel comfortable. We just get together here once a week to—'

She broke off as the hall doors were thrown open, and a

statuesque figure in a mohair jumper and leopard-print leggings rushed in.

'So sorry I'm late,' said Myrtle Duguid. 'My spinning class ran over, and I had to have a shower after it, and ... well, you know. But better late than never, eh?'

'We're pleased you could make it.'

Myrtle looked around in dismay – there was nowhere to sit. Benedict jumped up to offer his chair.

'Thank you,' she said. 'You're a gentleman.'

He went to fetch another chair from the stack in the corner, and everyone else shuffled round to make space for him.

'As I was saying to the rest of the group,' continued the Reverend when they'd settled again, 'this isn't a therapy—'

Myrtle burst into tears and put her hands over her face. Everyone looked at the Reverend in dismay. She put her arm around the sobbing woman.

'It's been so awful,' sobbed Myrtle. 'Just awful!'

The woman sitting on her other side handed her a tissue.

'Thank you.' Myrtle blew her nose. 'You can't begin to imagine how awful it's been!'

'Everyone here has lost someone,' said the Reverend gently. 'That's why we're all here.'

Myrtle nodded. 'Of course. Silly of me.' She blew her nose again.

'Not silly.' The Reverend gave her a comforting squeeze. 'Never silly. There's no right or wrong way to grieve. You just do what you can to get through.'

Liz wondered if the Reverend knew who Myrtle was, and if she was aware of the circumstances of Wally Duguid's death. There was an awkward silence.

'I remember when Kathy died,' volunteered Benedict. 'For weeks afterwards, I cycled. Miles and miles. Day and night. Anything rather than stay in the house on my own.'

Liz was surprised. Benedict had hardly mentioned his wife, Katherine, to her at all. It made her wonder just how well she knew him. Several people around the circle were nodding. Then the young woman sitting next to her spoke.

'When my sister Ann died last year,' she said, 'I didn't get out of bed for three weeks.'

She remembered the awful months after Mark died. She had thrown herself into her work, volunteering for extra shifts, until she'd accidentally mixed up two prescriptions. It was a relatively harmless mistake – thank goodness – but afterwards one of her colleagues had taken her aside to gently suggest she should take some time off. She'd never gone back. The Reverend was right. There was no single way grief could affect you, and no right way to deal with it.

Benedict fetched Myrtle a cup of tea while some of the others gathered round her. After that, they broke naturally into groups. Liz found herself having a conversation with the young woman about her dead sister and how her mum had reacted to her death. It wasn't fun, but it was surprisingly cathartic. She just wasn't sure if it was cathartic enough to make her come back again.

Afterwards, they stacked all the chairs and washed their own mugs. Benedict was hanging back, waiting for the Reverend to lock up so they could go to their squash game, so Liz waved goodbye to him and made her way out onto the street with some of the others. A leopard-spotted figure came out just behind them. On impulse, Liz approached her.

'It's Myrtle, isn't it? I'm Liz. Liz McLuckie. I'm so sorry about your husband. I don't suppose you fancy a drink?'

THE WHITE HORSE and Griffin wasn't as busy as Liz thought it would be on a Saturday night, and they were able to find a table in the narrow, dark-panelled front bar. Liz bought a half of lager for herself and a rum and Coke for Myrtle.

'You're an angel,' said Myrtle. 'I really need this.' She took a sip of her drink. 'I imagine you do, too. You're the one who found him, aren't you?'

There was no mistaking who she meant, and no ducking the answer. 'I'm afraid so.'

'I thought I recognised you. You came into the shop with your friend, didn't you? So lucky you both happened to be passing that night.'

Liz looked at her. The immaculately made-up face was completely guileless. Either Myrtle genuinely thought that she and Tilly had stumbled into the crime scene by accident, or she was the best actress in North Yorkshire. Myrtle took another sip and shook her head.

'I still can't get my head around him going like that.'

'It must have been a terrible shock.'

Myrtle snorted. 'One way of putting it.'

'The first few months are really hard,' said Liz. 'But it does get easier, I promise.'

'Easier?'

'The grief. It never leaves you completely, of course it doesn't, but it does get easier to—' Liz sought the right words '—deal with.'

Myrtle pulled a face and looked down at her drink. There was an awkward pause; then she peered back up at Liz through her eyelashes.

'You seem nice,' she said. 'Can I be honest with you?'

'Um … yes, of course.'

'It's not really Wally I'm grieving for.'

'Oh.'

'I recently lost someone else. Someone I loved very much.'

Of course. Ian Crowby.

'Wally and I ... well, we didn't really get on that well.'

'Ah.' Liz had no idea how best to respond to that.

'We were married fifteen years. A long time. But ... we weren't soul mates.' Myrtle snorted. 'Far from it. Let's just say I'm a butterfly, meant to live in the sun. To enjoy life, fluttering from flower to flower. Whereas Wally ...' She tailed off.

Liz still didn't know what to say, but didn't want to interrupt the flow of Myrtle's confidences, so just nodded sympathetically.

'Don't get me wrong,' continued Myrtle. 'Wally had his good points.' She paused. 'He was kind to animals. And was good to his mum before she died. Couldn't do enough for her, any time of the day or night. But ... he wasn't married to me ... not really ... he was married to his money.'

Liz tutted.

'Oh, I know it's not a nice thing to say about someone, but it's true.' Myrtle was on a roll now. 'Every penny was a hostage to him, as my old gran used to say. I had to beg him for every little thing ... housekeeping, clothes, even make-up. In the end, he insisted I got a part-time job. Completely humiliating.'

Liz made a noise she hoped sounded sympathetic.

'But Ian' – Myrtle brightened – 'was completely different. A real gentleman. If we went for a meal, he always paid for it, and he was so generous with other things too.' She held out her hand for Liz to admire. 'He bought me this only a few weeks ago.'

'Lovely.' Liz eyed the expensive-looking, if rather gaudy, cocktail ring. 'His death must have been a shock, too?'

'You have no idea. Both of them dead in less than a fortnight!'

'Just to be clear, it *is* Ian Crowby you're talking about?'

Myrtle nodded. 'My poor Ian. Dead as a doornail, up

there on the clifftop. It breaks my heart to think about him up there, all alone.'

Liz remembered that Janet had hinted her mother and father were planning to reconcile, and wondered whether it was true. If so, did Myrtle know about it? From the way she was talking, Liz imagined she didn't, but it couldn't hurt to be sure.

'Was Ian married, too?'

'Oh no ... Or rather he *was*, but separated. Very, very separated. I think it was only a matter of time ...' Myrtle broke off coyly.

'A matter of time ...?'

'Before he popped the question to me. We were in love.' Myrtle patted Liz's hand. 'This is nice, isn't it? I can't tell you how much of a relief it is to be able to talk to someone about all this.'

Liz wondered whether Myrtle didn't have any friends, and felt a pang of pity. She took a sip of her own drink, which she'd almost forgotten about.

'It can't be a coincidence, can it?' she said. 'Both of them being ... within a couple of weeks of each other?'

Myrtle shrugged. 'Who knows? The police don't seem to have a clue. Not about Wally, anyway. I'm not sure what's going on with poor Ian.'

'Didn't you wonder, when Ian was found, whether Wally might have ...?' Liz left the sentence dangling.

Myrtle choked on her rum and Coke. 'Killed him?' She hooted with laughter. Not entirely appropriate, thought Liz, under the circumstances. 'Wally wouldn't have had the guts for it. And, to be honest, he really didn't care that much. He knew about me and Ian, and I think he'd have been more bothered if I'd dropped one of his precious vases.' She hesitated before sharing her next confidence. 'There were times when I felt like going through that shop with a baseball bat.'

She closed her eyes and shivered. 'Oh, to hear the lovely sound of smashing glass and china!' She opened her eyes again. 'I had needs, you see. *Physical* needs. And Wally just wasn't interested in fulfilling them.'

Liz found herself speechless again. It turned out there was such a thing as too much information, but she supposed she'd been asking for it. She took a few more sips of her lager and saw that Myrtle had already finished her rum and Coke.

'What will you do now?' she asked her.

Myrtle sighed. 'I'm not sure. I just want to put it all behind me. When everything's settled, I might go abroad. I've always fancied Mallorca. All that sun and sangria.'

Liz was surprised. 'You're going to sell the shop?'

Myrtle gave her a look. 'Why wouldn't I? Horrible dusty old stuff. Not that I'll get much for it. The building's rented anyway, and we owe money on the stock. But I should get something from the life insurance.'

Liz said nothing. If Wally Duguid had been the kind of man to skimp on a security system, she didn't imagine he'd have been overly diligent with his insurance premiums. She hoped she was wrong, for Myrtle's sake.

The barman came past the table with an armful of empty glasses. He was a well-built young man, at least fifteen years younger than Myrtle. As he picked up Myrtle's empty glass, their eyes caught and held. He headed back to the bar.

Myrtle smirked. 'On the other hand,' she mused, 'I might stay here for a while. Whitby isn't without its attractions.' She glanced at the bar and saw the barman was still looking at her. She fluttered her eyelashes. Liz raised her eyebrows. Myrtle clearly didn't intend to wallow in grief for too long.

Myrtle stood up and smoothed her leggings over her hips. 'Well, this has been lovely, hasn't it? Let's do it again sometime.'

'Mm,' said Liz, hoping she looked more enthusiastic than

she felt. She'd hardly even started her lager. She decided she didn't want it anyway. 'I'll come out with you.' As she was picking up her handbag and cardigan, Myrtle darted her a sideways glance.

'I saw you talking to Benedict Ossett, in the support group. Is he a friend of yours?'

'Yes.'

'I've seen him around town, but only know him through Katherine, really. He's a lovely man, isn't he? A real gentleman.'

'I suppose so.' Whatever *that* was supposed to mean.

'And so attractive.'

Liz was stunned.

'Poor love. All alone in that big house. Ah well, you know what they say ... time heals all.' Myrtle smirked at Liz and headed out of the bar.

'It certainly does in your case,' muttered Liz as she followed. Outside on the pavement, they found themselves strobed by blue light. A police patrol car was pulled onto the pavement directly in front of the pub, lights spinning. Further down the alley, in White Horse Yard, they could hear voices and a commotion of some kind.

'I wonder what's going on,' said Liz.

'I don't know,' replied Myrtle. She looked agitated. 'But I don't want to get mixed up in any more funny business. See you around, Linda.'

18

Liz waited until Myrtle had hurried out of sight, then ducked into White Horse yard to see what was going on. Whatever it was, it seemed to be centred around Ian Crowby's cottage. The door was standing open, the lights were on, and she could hear the crackle of police radios inside. She was standing, wondering what to do next, when a figure emerged from the doorway. It jumped when it saw Liz.

'Oh, hello, Mrs McLuckie,' said Constable Williams. 'You gave me a bit of a fright there. What can I do for you?'

'I was just ... um ... passing. And I wondered what was going on.'

'Out for one of your strolls, eh?' There was a gleam in his eye that surprised her. She wondered whether his habitually mournful, lacklustre air might only be an act. She grinned at him.

'Something like that.'

Williams came to stand beside her. 'One of the neighbours heard noises inside. They knew the cottage was supposed to be empty, so they called it in.'

'Nothing serious, I hope.'

'Someone's given it a right going over.'

'Burgled, you mean?'

'We don't know if there's anything missing. We're waiting for the professor's daughter to get here.'

Another figure emerged from the cottage. Kevin did a double take when he saw Liz, and turned to Williams.

'The fingerprint team's due to arrive any minute, Bill. Do me a favour and make sure everything's ready for them?'

Williams nodded and went back inside.

Liz looked at Kevin. 'Bill?' she said. 'William Williams?'

Kevin smiled. 'They call him Cheap Seats at the station.'

Liz looked at him blankly.

'Double Bill?'

'Poor lad.'

'He handles it well enough.'

Liz nodded. That would explain the constable's careful camouflage of mildness. She looked at the brightly lit cottage. 'Do you think the thieves were after the girdle?'

'I doubt it. We went over the place pretty thoroughly when we heard it was missing, as well as Crowby's family house in York. If the girdle was in there, it was very well hidden, and I don't think whoever it was would have managed to find it in the time they had.'

'That doesn't mean it wasn't what they were looking for.'

'True.' Kevin rubbed his chin. 'Flint's on her way. You'd better make yourself scarce.'

'Okay.' Another run-in with the inspector was the last thing Liz wanted. 'I'll catch up with you later.'

As Kevin headed back inside, Liz made her way out through the dark alleyway to the street. Not wanting to jar her knee, she had to watch her footing carefully on the uneven cobbles. Just as she was about to step out onto the pavement, something bright caught her eye, wedged between two of the stones. She bent down to pick it up. It was an art deco hair-clip. A very *distinctive* art deco hairclip. There was no question who it belonged to. But had Dora dropped it the last time Liz had seen her in White Horse Yard? Or more recently?

'Oh, for the love of God.' There was no mistaking *that* voice. 'What are you doing here?'

Liz slipped the hair clip into her cardigan pocket and gave Inspector Flint what she hoped was an innocent look.

'Just passing, Inspector.'

Flint glared at her. 'Just passing? Do I have to remind you about our conversation the last time we spoke?'

'Of course not. I was just ...'

'Have you been in White Horse Yard?' Flint narrowed her eyes.

'I've been in the White Horse and Griffin.' That was true, but it didn't really answer the question Flint had asked. 'Why? Is there something going on?'

Flint gave her a sour look. 'Stay there.' She marched off into the alleyway. Liz lingered on the pavement, feeling conspicuous, until Flint returned about three minutes later, with Constable Williams in tow. She spoke to him without looking at Liz.

'I want you to drive Mrs McLuckie to the station and take a statement from her. I want to know everything she's done today, exactly when she did it. And I mean *everything*. I want to know everywhere she's been, everyone she's spoken to, and exactly what she's eaten.'

Williams opened his mouth to say something, but Flint cut across him.

'I don't care how long it takes. Just keep her out of my way.'

The constable hesitated. A mistake.

Flint glared at him. 'What are you bloody waiting for? Go!'

IT WAS GONE eleven and almost completely dark when Liz finally let herself into Kipper Cottage. Williams had taken Flint at her word and had taken pages and pages of notes on Liz's activities in the interview room at the station. He was meticulous, recording times, names and exact locations. Not that either of them really thought Flint suspected her of doing anything. They both knew she just wanted to teach Liz a lesson.

Now, Liz was exhausted. Unfortunately, she had to go straight back out again with Nelson, who had been keeping his legs crossed for hours and wasn't the least bit pleased about it. As soon as he'd relieved himself on a bollard, he made a point of ignoring her, not even thawing when they got home and she gave him his favourite tinned fish. She couldn't say she blamed him. She had abandoned him at the café, then left him for hours on his own. That neglect, combined with having inflicted Dora Spackle on him the week before *and* having locked him in the understairs cupboard, meant it was hardly surprising their relationship was hanging by a thread. As soon as he'd finished his supper, he got into his basket and turned his back on her.

Liz sighed and looked round the kitchen. Most of the furniture was still upstairs, but at least she no longer had to pick her way through the glue on the floor, thanks to the miracle Niall had performed with the sandblaster. The stone was completely clean apart from a fine film of dust that Liz guessed would be there for many days to come, no matter how many times she used the vacuum. She groaned as she remembered her vacuum cleaner had broken just before she'd got ready for the support group. She needed to buy a new one, or she'd be forever on her knees with a dustpan and brush, something she was keen to avoid. Her knee was as painful as it had ever been, throbbing and fiery. She hobbled up the stairs to find her pyjamas and some painkillers.

She was in bed in less than five minutes. She intended to sleep for as long as possible. A week, if she could. But once she'd turned off the light, her eyes stayed wide, wide open. She heard St Mary's bell chime the half hour on the clifftop, and found herself thinking about Myrtle Duguid and the conversation they'd had in the bar. It wasn't the intimacies of the Duguids' marriage that occupied her thoughts – thankfully – but Myrtle's last throwaway comments about Benedict. She'd been shocked and slightly horrified by her own instinctive reaction to it. She was jealous.

She'd tried to deny it for as long as she could, but perhaps it was time for her to admit that her feelings for Benedict had gone beyond the boundaries of friendship. She wasn't sure exactly when or how that had happened, but now she found herself in the unlooked-for and entirely astonishing position of being attracted to someone other than Mark.

The question was, was she prepared to act on it? She didn't think so. She didn't think it was an option, anyway. Benedict had never given her any reason to think he saw her as anything other than a friend. He treated her exactly the same way he treated Tilly – with consideration and good humour, nothing more. And even if he was interested in her that way, could she really be bothered with all the intricacies and rituals of sexual relations again? All that fuss and exertion. All that interminable *grooming*?

Even as she asked herself those questions, she knew she was being disingenuous. If Benedict ever did make a pass at her, she was pretty sure she'd grab the opportunity – and him – with both hands. There was something about him that just seemed to bypass her usual defences.

Scratch, scratch, scratch.

Liz listened in disbelief. Nelson had only just been outside. Surely he didn't need to go out again? She was lovely and warm, feeling sleepy at last. If she kept very, very quiet, he might ...

Scratch, scratch, SCRATCH!

Oh, dear God. She swung her legs out of bed and winced as she put her feet on the floor. Her knee felt about twice its usual size. She couldn't be bothered to get dressed, so decided just to put a coat on over her pyjamas. There'd be no one around to see her at that time of night.

Downstairs, Nelson greeted her with a wag of his tail.

'So *now* you want to talk to me, do you? Now you've got me out of bed. Bloody animal.' She didn't have the heart to be really cross with him – when a dog's got to go, a dog's got to go. She pulled her anorak on, slipped her feet into her wellies, clipped Nelson on his lead and let herself out of the cottage.

Henrietta Street was completely deserted, its white-washed cottages ghostly in the moonlight. She hoped Nelson could hold his bladder until they got to one of the ghauts on Church Street – the narrow alleyways that cut down to the shore. She didn't like to let him relieve himself on the street if she could help it. Nelson knew that and kept darting her anxious glances, but they weren't making very fast progress, thanks to her knee. Eventually, he decided he couldn't wait and came to an immovable halt. He cocked his leg against the wall of one of the shops. Liz was too knackered to stop him.

'Ah, the joys of pet ownership.'

Liz looked up, dismayed. Reverend Garraway was grinning at her, her sports bag over her shoulder. Her hair was damp, and she wore no make-up. She looked about sixteen.

'Ha, ha. Yes.' Liz's laugh sounded forced, even to her.

Liz tugged at Nelson's lead, but he refused to budge. He was still peeing.

'You wouldn't think this was the second time he's been out tonight.' She said, embarrassed.

'Needs must when the devil drives.'

'Ha, ha. Yes.'

The Reverend continued to smile at her, not seeming in any hurry to continue on her way. Liz assumed she was going home, wherever that was. She didn't think it was on the clifftop by the church. Maybe it was somewhere near the steps? Liz took in the implication of the sports bag. The Reverend hadn't been home since her game with Benedict. Where had she been all this time? At Benedict's?

Nelson finally dropped his leg and gave a happy little sigh.

'Finished?' she asked him. 'Can we go home now?'

'You live on Henrietta Street, don't you?' said the Reverend.

'Yes. Kipper Cottage, beside the smokehouse.'

'I'm on the shore, behind the Duke of York. Mind if I walk with you?'

'Not at all. As long as you don't mind taking it slowly.'

The Reverend saw Liz's limp as they walked. 'Oh dear, what have you done?'

'Nothing too bad. Just twisted a ligament in my knee. The doctor says I need physiotherapy, but I haven't got round to sorting it yet.'

'You should. You can't be too careful with knees.' The Reverend chuckled. 'What you need is St Ælfflaed's girdle.'

'Sorry?'

'St Ælfflaed's girdle.'

'I don't follow you.'

'For your knee.'

Liz still didn't get it. The Reverend saw her puzzled

expression and laughed. 'Haven't you heard of St Ælfflaed's girdle? It was a present from St Cuthbert to Ælfflaed, Abbess of Whitby.'

'Yes, I've heard of it. How would it help my knee?'

'Just before St Ælfflaed received it, she'd been suffering terribly from some crippling disease. Probably arthritis – she must have been well into old age by then. She prayed to God for help, and the next day got the girdle from Cuthbert. She put it on, and the pain miraculously disappeared.'

Liz had stopped walking. 'It has healing powers?'

'Supposedly.' The Reverend pulled a face. 'Of course, even as a Christian, you have to take these things with a pinch of salt.'

Nelson tugged on his lead, prompting Liz to start walking again.

The Reverend continued cheerfully. 'The medieval era was teeming with miraculous artifacts. Nails from the cross. Jesus's sandals. Holy sponges. Holy thorns ... Not to mention all the mummified body parts and bones of the saints. St John the Evangelist has at least three tombs that I know of.'

'But people do believe in these things?'

'They do.' The Reverend looked thoughtful. 'Of course, it's not so much the objects themselves as what they represent. It's so tempting to be worldly-wise and cynical in this modern world of ours, with all our technology and scientific knowledge, but we should never underestimate the power of faith.'

'I suppose not.'

The Reverend halted suddenly. 'This is me.'

Liz saw they'd reached the Duke of York.

'It was so nice to see you at the support group tonight,' said the Reverend. 'I hope you'll come again?'

The question caught Liz by surprise. 'Um ... maybe.'

The other woman nodded and smiled. They both knew what that really meant. 'Night, then.'

Liz watched her disappear down the lane beside the pub, ignoring Nelson, who was tugging at his lead. Now that he'd emptied his bladder, he was desperate to get back to his basket. But Liz lingered, her thoughts tumbling.

If St Ælfflaed's girdle had healing powers – or even the *reputation* for healing powers – the theft might have nothing to do with money at all.

And neither might the murders.

19

'It's still too sloppy,' said Niall. 'I can't get it to stay put.'

'Hang on a minute.' Liz put down her screwdriver and went to the bag of plaster in the middle of the kitchen floor. She tipped some into the bucket Niall was using, and gave it a buzz with the handheld mixer. She watched, sweating, as Niall scooped some of the new mix onto his trowel. 'Any better?'

'Yeah, I think so.' He swiped the trowel experimentally across the wall. 'Yeah. Much better.'

'I didn't want to make it too dry, or it wouldn't last five minutes.'

It was unseasonably hot for early June. Even though Niall was only wearing shorts, his hair was limp with sweat as he filled in the holes where the wood panelling had been screwed and glued to the kitchen walls. Liz was wearing the only sundress she owned, not especially practical for DIY, but at least it had the benefit of not constricting her knee as she replaced all the broken light switches with new ones.

Nelson lay on the stone floor and panted. It was too hot for Yorkshire. Which reminded Liz ...

'How's it going with your application for the Athens dig?'

Niall wiped his arm across his forehead and looked glum. 'Not great. They've asked for references from my most recent employer. I've said I'll try, but I know I'm wasting my time even asking. There's no way I'm going to get a reference from Dora Spackle.'

Nelson growled.

'I love that feckin' dog,' said Niall.

'Isn't there anyone else you could ask?'

'There would have been if the prof hadn't been murdered.'

'Inconvenient of him.'

'Too right.'

'What will you do if you can't get a place?'

'Well, I can always try to get a place on an unpaid dig next summer, but I'll have to work really hard through the winter to be able to afford it. And there's still no guarantee I'll get a place. It's very competitive.'

'For an unpaid position? That doesn't seem fair.'

Niall shrugged. 'It is what it is.' He stood back and admired his handiwork. 'This is going on a treat. It should only take about an hour, I reckon. I might even get it sanded today.'

'What time does your shift start at the pub?' she asked.

'Not 'til five. What are your plans for the rest of the day, Mrs Mac?'

Liz wiped a hand across her brow. 'Actually, I'm going on a little trip.'

'Anywhere nice?'

'Middlesbrough.'

'Cool.'

'Let's hope so.' What had seemed like a good idea when she'd woken up that morning didn't seem quite so brilliant now. The idea of getting on a hot train with lots of other sweating people really wasn't very appealing, and then she would have to catch a taxi at the other end – all for something that might very well turn out to be a complete waste of time. She glanced at the clock. She needed to take a shower now if she wanted to catch the train. She finished putting the last screw in the new switch and put all the old yellowing plastic switches into the rubbish bag.

'That's me done. Is it okay if I leave you in charge?'

Niall saluted. 'Aye, aye, Captain. I'll take Nelson out just before I go.'

'He'll be okay for a couple of hours. I should be back by seven, if everything goes to plan.'

Not that there was a plan. Or not much of one, anyway. What she intended to do was to catch a train to Middlesbrough and then take a taxi to the James Cook University Hospital, where she would do nothing more sophisticated than hanging around the entrance, waiting for Professor Crowby's daughter, Janet, to either start or finish her shift. There was a more than even chance that she wouldn't see her at all.

As plans went, it was actually pretty rubbish, but it was the best she could think of, for now. When she'd retrieved Janet's business card from Iris that morning, she'd thought about simply ringing Janet and asking if they could meet up for a coffee. But then she'd have to have a reason for wanting to talk to her. She did have a reason, of course, but it wasn't one she wanted to share with Janet up front. She wanted to catch her off guard. Which was sneaky and unfair, but necessary.

After talking to Reverend Garraway the night before, Liz had hobbled slowly home. The fact that St Ælfflaed's girdle supposedly had healing powers had made her think. What might someone do for a miracle cure? Kill? Quite probably. They would certainly pay a *lot* of money for one. It seemed that everything still came down to money in the end, but the motivations could be quite different than she had imagined. After settling Nelson back in his basket, she'd returned thoughtfully to her own bed.

Was there someone connected to Ian Crowby or Wally Duguid who might benefit from a religious relic with healing properties? Someone involved in healthcare, perhaps?

It didn't take a genius to work it out.

THE TRAIN JOURNEY from Whitby to the town of Middlesbrough was a scenic one, particularly beautiful on a summer day. First of all, the train ran through the wooded valley of the river Esk, crossing and recrossing the water over a succession of bridges before climbing up onto the moorland of the North York Moors National Park. The moor had its own bleak beauty, its horizon studded with hills, including the local beauty spot Roseberry Topping, a distinctive escarpment that looked like a shark's fin. After an hour and a quarter, the rural landscape surrendered to urban, to the yards and warehouses of the busy industrial outskirts of Middlesbrough.

There were quite a few taxis waiting at the station when Liz arrived. To her dismay, when she told the driver she wanted to go to James Cook University Hospital, he asked her which entrance she wanted. She had no idea.

'The oncology department? I'm not sure exactly where that is.' MacMillan nurses like Janet were specialists in cancer care.

The driver gave her a look of sympathy in the rear-view mirror and nodded. On the drive to the hospital, Liz thought about Wendy, who had been Mark's MacMillan nurse during his last couple of weeks in the hospice. She had been a tower of strength, explaining everything about his palliative care and pain medication, giving emotional support and guidance to them both when they needed it. In the last couple of days, after Mark had lapsed into unconsciousness, Wendy had always seemed to be around to put a comforting hand on Liz's shoulder, or appear as if by magic with a cup of tea when she was at her most despairing. In the brief contact Liz had had with Janet in her father's cottage in White Horse Yard, she had seemed similarly strong and empathetic. Was Liz really going to accuse her of ... what, exactly? Of exploiting a religious relic for personal gain? It seemed completely ridiculous when she put it like that.

In less than twenty minutes, she had arrived at the hospital, a sprawling modern red-brick building on the outskirts of the town. She found a bench where she could see the entrance clearly, and made herself comfortable. It didn't take her long to realise, however, that no one coming in or out was wearing a uniform. Was there a separate staff entrance?

She did a circuit of the building, slowly because of her knee, and spotted a staff car park. There was an unmarked entrance into the hospital nearby, with a steady flow of people coming in and out, like a beehive. Some of them were wearing scrubs. Bingo. She found a bench in the shade, close enough to be able to see people's faces clearly, and settled herself again. She'd brought plenty of water and snacks with her. She reckoned she could stay about four hours if she had to. She really hoped that wouldn't be necessary, but was beginning to realise it probably would be. There was no guarantee Janet hadn't worked an earlier shift and had already been and gone. Or that she was going to work a late shift and wouldn't arrive until after Liz had to leave. Or that Janet was working that day at all. Liz's whole day was likely to be in vain. Stupid.

But she was here now.

The first hour passed fairly quickly, but after that, time started to drag. Liz couldn't even distract herself with a book

– she had to stay alert, scanning the faces of the steady flow of people coming in and out. Her mind wandered. Occasionally it wandered to Benedict, but whenever it did, she pushed it somewhere else. There was no point thinking about him. The sun moved gradually across the sky, until Liz realised her face was stinging. She'd been sitting in full sunshine. She moved to a different bench in the shade, but it wasn't quite as well placed for people-watching. The car park was behind her now, so that she couldn't see faces until they were closer to the entrance.

She'd been there more than three hours and had just unwrapped a sandwich when she spotted Janet. She didn't recognise her at first. She looked different in her uniform, with her hair pulled back into a ponytail and wearing glasses. She'd emerged from the car park and was heading quickly for the door.

'Janet!' Liz dropped her sandwich to wave. 'JANET!'

The other woman looked round and did a double take when she spotted Liz. Liz jumped up and went over to her.

'Hello,' said Janet doubtfully. 'It's Mrs McLuckie, isn't it?'

'Liz.'

'I didn't recognise you at first. What are you doing here?'

'I'm … um … visiting a friend.'

Janet frowned. Liz guessed she was wondering why she'd been sitting at the staff entrance.

'I got a bit lost. The hospital's so big.'

Janet's brow cleared, and she nodded.

'How are you?' asked Liz. 'Did Iris get in touch? About the cleaning? I gave her your card.'

Janet nodded. 'She's going to help me. Thank you for recommending her. She seems very capable.'

They grinned at each other. Janet looked at her watch. 'I am a bit early. We can grab a coffee if you like?'

The staff cafeteria was quite busy, with many nurses,

doctors and porters taking their breaks. Quite a few were eating, even though it was too late for lunch and too early for dinner. Liz supposed they just had to take the opportunity to grab something whenever they could get it. Janet insisted on buying the drinks. She gave Liz a mug of tea and sat down opposite her.

'It's not great, I'm afraid.' She grinned. 'Sometimes we use it as an antiseptic.'

'As long as it's hot and wet, I'm sure it's fine.' Liz took a sip and revised that opinion. She put the mug down again.

'Has your friend been here long?' asked Janet.

Liz looked at her.

'The friend you're visiting?'

Liz shook her head. 'Oh. No. Not long.'

'Nothing too serious, I hope?' Janet looked genuinely interested as she sipped her coffee.

'Not at all ... not serious. Thankfully.'

'Which ward are they in?'

'You must have to deal with a lot of desperate people in your job,' stuttered Liz.

'Sorry?' Janet was surprised at the abrupt change of subject.

Liz realised how peculiar that must have sounded. '*Desperate* is maybe the wrong word ... Beyond hope?'

Janet pulled a face. 'I don't think anyone is ever beyond hope. Not really. Even at the end.'

Liz nodded. It was part of what made humans human. 'I suppose it helps if you're religious,' she said.

'I think it does. Many of my patients turn to God in their last days. Even ones who'd never really bothered before.'

Liz wondered how best to continue, and decided a direct approach was as good as any. She watched Janet's face carefully.

'Did your father ever mention St Ælfflaed's girdle to you?'

'What?'

'St Ælfflaed's girdle.'

'What's that?' She looked genuinely puzzled.

'A relic they have ... they *had* ... at the museum. It has healing powers.'

Janet raised her eyebrows.

'I imagine that would come in very handy in your line of work,' said Liz.

'Well, yes ... it would. If ...'

'I imagine people might be prepared to pay a lot of money for a miracle.'

Janet put down her coffee with a frown. 'I'm sorry. What is it you're asking me, exactly?'

'The girdle went missing from the museum just before your father died.'

Realisation dawned.

'You think *I* have it?'

'I think your father might have.'

'You're saying he *stole* it?' Janet's face was getting redder. 'From the museum?'

Liz's expression betrayed her.

'What is *wrong* with you people? Ever since dad died, you think it gives you the right to say the most spiteful, horrible things about him.'

Liz was dismayed by the turn the conversation was taking. 'I'm sorry, I never ...'

'Less than a week after he died, that horrible woman from the museum marched right into the cottage and told me he'd been having an affair with his friend's wife.'

Dora. Liz was shocked. That must have been the day she saw her coming out of White Horse Yard. What a spiteful thing to do! No wonder Janet had been crying.

'That was just before you turned up.' Janet's eyes opened wider. 'Oh my God! You don't have a friend here at all, do you?' Her voice was rising, prompting people at some of the other tables to turn to look. 'You've just doorstepped me to make this horrible accusation.'

'It's not like that,' protested Liz. But even as she said it, a little voice inside her said it was *exactly* like that.

'I thought you were nice.' Janet stood up. 'But you're just the same. You're just as horrible as everyone else in that narrow-minded little town. You should be ashamed of yourself.'

'I'm sorry, I just ...'

But Janet didn't let her finish. She turned and strode out of the cafeteria, leaving Liz with her mouth open. Liz saw people were looking at her. Her face flamed. She managed to hold herself together until she got into a taxi, but cried all the way back to the station. The driver maintained a tactful silence, no doubt thinking she'd just lost someone at the hospital. He was right, in a way. But she hadn't lost someone, she'd lost *something*.

Her self-respect.

By the time she arrived back at Kipper Cottage a couple of hours later, she'd never been so glad to get anywhere in her life. Nelson greeted her with a yip and a wag of his tail as she dumped her bag on the floor and took her coat off. He looked startled when she flung her arms around his neck. She clung to him and sobbed into his fur.

How had she come to this? How could she accuse Janet – a woman who had selflessly dedicated her life to helping others – of such a terrible thing? It had nothing to do with her anyway. None of it did. The girdle. The murders. How had she turned into such a busybody? Was her life really so barren and uneventful she had to live it second-hand and find some kind of entertainment in something as horrible as murder? What would Mark think of the woman she'd become? Would he even recognise her? It was all too awful to think about.

Eventually, Nelson decided he'd had enough. He wriggled out of her grasp and went to stand pointedly beside his food bowl. Liz wiped her face.

Life went on ...

20

The next morning, Liz woke with a steely new resolution. She would forget about the murders and the girdle and Benedict Bloody Ossett and concentrate on putting her own house in order. Literally and metaphorically. The kitchen in Kipper Cottage looked like a building site – bereft of furniture, covered in sand and plaster dust, with patched walls and grubby paintwork. The inglenook, as lovely as she knew it was going to be one day, yawned in the centre like a cavernous mouth.

She would sort everything out by concentrating on one thing at a time. By doing that, and nothing but that, she might squash her unlovely tendency to dabble in other people's business.

After she'd got dressed and had walked Nelson on the shore, she hobbled over the bridge to Baxtergate, bought a new Hoover and several tins of emulsion paint, and brought it all back by taxi. Then she changed into her overalls, turned Diana Ross and the Supremes up full volume and set to work.

First, she vacuumed. She vacuumed and vacuumed, emptied the bag, then vacuumed some more. Then she mopped the worktops and the floor, tipping bucket after bucket of mucky water down the drain. After that, she called Ryan Goddard, who promised to come and take away the old kitchen cooker that afternoon. Then she made herself a cup of tea and switched on her laptop. She ordered a brand new Aga-style cooker and found a rather lovely second-hand woodburning stove for the inglenook from someone in Scarborough who was renovating their grandmother's house. She arranged to collect the wood burner the next day, and managed to find someone local who agreed to come and fit it the following week.

When all that was done, she found her stepladders and opened a can of emulsion paint.

'Oh my God,' said Niall, three hours later, when he stuck his head into the cottage. 'Have I come to the wrong cottage by mistake?'

Liz turned the music down. 'I've been busy.'

'I can see that.'

The kitchen was completely dust-free, its worktops and stone-flagged floor gleaming. Liz had put one coat of 'Old White' emulsion on the walls, and it had already made a world of difference, lightening and brightening the whole room. While she was waiting for the first coat to dry, she'd started on the woodwork.

'Don't touch that door frame,' she warned Niall. 'It's wet. Is there something you wanted?'

Niall seemed surprised by her question. 'I just ... erm ... wondered if you needed anything at the shop.'

'I'm fine, thanks.'

'Do you want a hand with anything?'

'No, I'm fine. Perfectly fine.'

'What about Nelson?' The bull terrier was sitting in his basket with the bewildered air of Toto, the dog from *The*

Wizard of Oz, caught up in a tornado. 'Would he like to come to the shop with me?'

Nelson, catching the general drift of the conversation, wagged his tail.

'Looks like it,' said Liz. 'I'll get his lead. It's in this lot somewhere.'

She rummaged on the floor, in the pile of stuff she'd taken off the walls so she could paint them, and found the lead wrapped around the sailing ship poker she'd got from Wally Duguid. While she was clipping the lead onto Nelson's collar, Niall shot her a searching look.

'What?' she asked. 'Do I have paint on my face?'

'Yes,' said Niall. 'But it's not that.'

She scrubbed at her cheeks. 'What is it, then?'

'Are you okay?'

'Why?'

'You just seem ... different.'

'I am. I'm better.'

'Your knee, you mean?'

'No. That's still knackered.'

'So ... better in what way?'

'Every way.' She beamed at him. 'Every possible way.'

'I didn't think there was anything else wrong with you.'

'Well, there was. But it's better now. Completely better.' She gleamed at him again.

'Okay.' Niall looked at her sideways. 'If you say so.' He headed for the door and was just about to open it when someone knocked. It was Ryan Goddard.

'Here for the cooker,' he announced unnecessarily.

'Do you need to disconnect it first?' asked Liz.

'No. I did that the last time I was here.' He grinned. 'Just in case you weren't listening when I told you not to use it.'

'Sneaky,' said Liz.

'Whatever it takes to keep my customers safe,' said Ryan.

'I'll give you a hand.' Niall handed Nelson's lead to Liz. It only took a few minutes for the two men to wrestle the old cooker out of the kitchen and into the van that Ryan had reversed down the street.

'I'll send you an invoice for the dump fee, Mrs M,' Ryan called, then drove off, with the stove rattling and clanking inside the van. Niall retrieved Nelson and took off too, leaving Liz staring at the mucky gap where the cooker used to be.

She felt deflated suddenly and not a little exhausted. But her plan had worked. She'd been so busy she hadn't given a thought to murder, medieval artifacts or middle-aged romance for hours and hours. All in all, she decided, it had been a very satisfying kind of day.

THE NEXT DAY, she continued her campaign of staying too busy to think. She rented a van and went to pick up the woodburning stove in Scarborough. Scarborough was another seaside town about twenty miles down the coast, quite different in feel and appearance to Whitby. Whitby was primarily a fishing town, but Scarborough, in its heyday, had been a very grand tourist resort. People used to come from all over the North of England in steam trains, charabancs and omnibuses to stroll in the town's pleasure gardens and paddle in the shallows of its two gorgeous beaches. Like most Victorian resorts, it had taken a bit of a beating in the latter half of the twentieth century. Even though its popularity had remained high with ordinary working people, its more affluent visitors had abandoned it in favour of the south of France and the Caribbean. It was still well loved, however, and in recent years had been undergoing something of a renaissance. Many of its Victorian and Georgian properties were enjoying facelifts and full renovations. The house on St Sepulchre Street, where she was due to collect the wood burner, was easy to spot because of the scaffolding and rubbish skip outside. She couldn't resist having a peek in the skip and spotted two old chapel chairs. After she'd negotiated a fair price for the wood burner, she asked about the chairs. The owner, who had intended throwing them away, let her take them for free.

When everything was safely loaded into the van, and money had changed hands, Liz got in and started the engine. It was another beautiful day. It seemed a pity to go straight home. Should she take a stroll around Peasholm Park, the town's Japanese pleasure gardens?

Her mobile rang, startling her out of her thoughts. The caller ID said it was Benedict. She dismissed the call with a flash of irritation. That was the third time he'd called since Saturday. And the third time she'd let it go to answerphone. Bubble burst, she decided to head straight home. With its lake and ducks and fairy lights, Peasholm Park was far too romantic to visit alone.

Niall helped her to unload the wood burner at the other end before starting his afternoon shift at the Duke of York. She returned the car to the hire shop and caught a taxi home. She planned to put a second coat of emulsion on the walls, but she couldn't face it straightaway. She made herself a cup of tea instead and drank it perched on one of her new chapel chairs. She was very pleased with the chairs, which were made from pine and had racks on the back for Bibles. She knew they would clean up rather nicely, but was struggling to feel as pleased about that as she ought to be. Perhaps she was just tired?

Nelson came and sat at her feet, as if sensing her mood. She realised her current constant state of frenetic activity wasn't sustainable. Apart from anything else, her body wasn't up to it: Her muscles were aching from getting up and down the stepladder and heaving the wood burner stove around, and her knee had stiffened up almost completely. She would have to revise her plan of painting that afternoon, but what could she do instead that was constructive and would take her mind off other people's business? She searched her jeans pocket and found the card Dr Prakash had given her.

The receptionist took several rings to answer.

'Good afternoon, Eskmouth Physiotherapy and Pain Management, how can I help you?'

Liz knew that voice. She hung up in surprise. To be fair, Myrtle Duguid had told her she had a part-time job, but Liz had assumed it was in Wally's shop. She hadn't realised it was at the physiotherapists. Why had it shocked her so much?

Was there someone connected to Ian Crowby or Wally Duguid who might benefit from a religious relic with healing properties?

Liz pushed the thought away. It was none of her business. *None of my business.*

'Damn it,' she muttered. She got up and went to get her overalls. Nelson slunk back into his basket as she covered the floor with dust sheets and fetched her stepladder. She prised a paint can open.

Was there someone connected to Ian Crowby or Wally Duguid who might benefit from a religious relic with healing properties?

Liz barely saw the walls as she slapped paint on them. Instead, in her mind's eye, Myrtle Duguid's cocktail ring blinded her with its gaudy glitter. Thirty payments of three hundred pounds.

'Damn. Damn. Damn.'

She covered the walls faster than she had the day before, working like a dervish. Afterwards, she didn't bother pausing to inspect her handiwork, but hurried instead to roll up the dust sheets and put the immersion heater on for a shower.

It was no good. She had to know for sure.

. . .

ALTHOUGH IT WAS LATE AFTERNOON, it was still sunny outside, and the air felt exceptionally humid. There was either a thunderstorm coming, or they were in for fog. Fog in Whitby was often spectacular, thick enough to cut with a knife, but more often occurred in the autumn. If unseasonal fog was on the way, Liz hoped she'd get back to Kipper Cottage before it made an appearance.

Church Street was its usual noisy self, busy with families and old-age pensioners on day trips, oblivious to the impending weather. As Liz hobbled through the crowd, she spotted a face coming towards her that she knew. Dora Spackle pretended she hadn't seen her, and hurried past without acknowledgement. Liz hesitated, then came to a decision.

'Dora!' she called out after her.

Dora stopped. Liz hurried to join her as fast as her knee allowed.

'What is it?' snapped Dora, eyes hostile behind her glasses. 'I'm in a hurry.'

'I have something belonging to you.' Liz rummaged in her cardigan pocket, hoping it was still there. It was. She gave Dora her hair clip. 'You dropped this.'

Dora looked surprised, but took the clip.

'You dropped it in White Horse Yard. The question is,' continued Liz, 'did you lose it when you went to tell Janet Baxter about her father's affair with Myrtle Duguid? Or later, when you broke into the cottage to get your letters?'

Dora darted a horrified glance around the busy street. No one was taking any notice of their conversation.

'I don't know what you mean,' she muttered.

'I think you do.'

The look on Dora's face told Liz everything she needed to know.

'Jealousy is a terrible thing,' said Liz. 'It eats away at you, bit by bit, until there's nothing left.'

Dora said nothing, but her eyes were suddenly suspiciously bright.

'You were in love with Ian Crowby,' said Liz.

Still, Dora remained silent.

Liz continued, relentless. 'It's nothing to be ashamed of. We've all been the victim of unrequited love at one time or another.' Benedict's face rose unbidden in her mind. 'But you really shouldn't have told Janet about Myrtle. That was unnecessary and spiteful.'

'I could have waited,' whispered Dora. 'I could have been happy, just loving him and saying nothing. He was married. But then *she* came. With her hair ... and her body.' She shook her head bitterly. 'And it turned out he was just like every other man.'

'People on pedestals almost always take a tumble,' said Liz. 'You wasted your time looking for the letters, though. The police have them.'

'The police?'

'They found them not long after he was killed.'

'You won't ... you won't tell them, will you?' Dora's voice wasn't much more than a whisper. 'That I wrote them? That I broke in?'

Liz hesitated. Her instinct was to immediately reassure Dora that she wouldn't, but she stopped herself. She was being far too nice. Dora didn't deserve peace of mind. Not yet, anyway.

'I don't know,' said Liz. 'I haven't decided.'

'Isn't there *anything* I can do to persuade you?'

A thought occurred to Liz. Dora sensed it and jumped on it eagerly. 'There is something, isn't there? Whatever it is, I'll do it!'

. . .

LIZ ARRIVED at the physiotherapists on the West Cliff about half an hour later. It was on the ground floor of one of the big Edwardian buildings overlooking the sea, with a frosted bay window and a polished sign beside the door that said Eskmouth Physiotherapy. Liz lifted her chin and went inside. The waiting room was empty apart from Myrtle Duguid, who sat behind the reception desk, wearing a white coat over a pink lace blouse and leggings. Her eyes opened wide when she saw Liz.

'Linda,' she said, 'what a surprise!'

'It's Liz, actually. Do you have a few minutes for a chat?'

'What about?'

Emboldened by the success of her direct approach with Dora Spackle, Liz decided to go for it.

'About your scam with Ian Crowby. The one with the girdle.'

Myrtle's lipsticked mouth formed a perfect O. She blinked once, twice, then glanced at the clock on the wall. It was almost 6 pm.

'I'm nearly done here. I'll meet you at the Copper Kettle café in five minutes ... if that's okay?'

Liz nodded briskly and headed out again. That had gone better than she could have hoped.

The Copper Kettle was a few hundred yards further along the West Cliff, close to the hugely popular art deco paddling pool. Only twelve inches deep, the pool provided a safe environment for toddlers and somewhere shady for parents, grannies and grandads to sit. The façade of the Copper Kettle was painted cream and green, the same as the curvaceous public toilets beside the pool. Inside, it had a similar art deco vibe, with glossy tiles and curved tables. There was only one other customer in the café, an elderly man with a terrier – at that time of day most of the pool-going families had headed back to their accommodation to feed their little ones and put them to bed. Which was probably why Myrtle had chosen the Copper Kettle for their *tete-a-tete*.

Liz ordered a pot of tea from the elaborately moustachioed barista and wondered whether she'd been wise to have confronted Myrtle so openly. Or Dora, for that matter. She decided it wasn't too much of a risk. Whoever had killed Ian Crowby had been strong enough to lift him up to the font, plus she didn't really think that either Dora or Myrtle was a killer. She was convinced Crowby's death was connected with the girdle, though. She just didn't know how.

Liz caught her thoughts. So much for not getting involved with other people's business! She had to admit she'd had a fright with Janet at the hospital, and the episode had revealed a side of herself she wasn't particularly proud of. But was it really *so* bad? She had a healthy curiosity about people. She'd tried to distract it and squash it down, but that hadn't worked. It was as much a part of her as her curly hair or her sideways sense of humour. So rather than wishing it away, perhaps she should harness it instead and use it to put things right with Janet and help Kevin keep his job?

Myrtle's arrival interrupted her thoughts. Pink in the face and flustered, she ordered a latte at the counter and took a seat in the booth opposite Liz. Liz could tell just how agitated she was by the fact she hadn't flirted with the barista. They stared across the table at each other like gunslingers, waiting to see who would speak first.

'Okay.' Myrtle eventually held up her hands in a gesture of surrender. 'I admit it. We had the girdle.'

'How did it work? The scam?'

'I would identify patients at the clinic who I knew were Christian ... people with chronic or terminal illnesses, who might be interested in a potential "cure".' Myrtle made dismissive speech marks in the air as she said it. 'Then we'd charge them for five minutes' treatment.'

'How much did you charge?' Liz already knew the answer, but wanted the other woman to say it.

'Three hundred pounds.' Myrtle didn't even have the grace to look ashamed. 'They would have paid more, I think, but we didn't want to be greedy.'

Liz snorted. 'Decent of you.' She had a thought. 'Did you keep a list?'

'Eh?'

'A list of patients.'

'Oh, yes. Ian carried it around with him. Said he didn't want it falling into the wrong hands.'

One mystery solved. The missing fish wrapper. Was the killer on the list? Was that why he'd taken it?

'How long were you doing the treatments?'

'About eight months. We always knew it was a short-term thing. We hadn't stolen the girdle, just borrowed it. Ian always said he'd put it back in the museum eventually, but ...' She hesitated.

'But you liked the money too much?'

Myrtle shook her head. 'It wasn't that.'

She fell silent as the barista appeared at their table with their tea and coffee. Liz waited until he was out of earshot again.

'So what was it?'

'Wally. He found the girdle in one of my drawers. He recognised it straight away and made me confess what was going on. He told us he wanted a slice of the action. Suggested we put all the transactions through his companies so no one could trace it back to Ian. For a percentage, of course.'

'Of course.'

'So that's what we did, for a while.' Myrtle sighed. 'But Wally wasn't satisfied. He said he couldn't understand why we were bothering with a few hundred quid here and there when the girdle was worth thousands to the right buyer.'

'And what did Ian say?'

'He wasn't happy. Not at all. But what could he do? Wally threatened to tell the police if he didn't agree to sell it. He even had someone lined up who was willing to pay top price.'

Liz supposed it wouldn't be too hard for someone with contacts in the antiques trade to find that kind of buyer. Tears spiked Myrtle's lashes as she stirred her coffee. Liz almost felt sorry for her. Almost.

'So then what happened?'

'Ian decided to put the girdle back. I think he was on his way to do it when he was murdered.'

'You're sure it wasn't Wally who killed him?'

'Why would he? He had no idea Ian was going to put the girdle back. Plus, Wally really was a hopeless ...' Myrtle stopped herself before she could speak ill of the dead. 'No. I think it must have been the buyer. The one Wally had lined up. Why pay thousands for something when you can take it for nothing?'

Liz supposed that made sense. They were silent for a few moments. Myrtle sipped her coffee, face grim.

'You have to go to the police,' said Liz.

Myrtle almost choked. 'Are you *kidding*?'

'You have to tell them everything. About the girdle. Charging people for treatment. The buyer.'

'I can't.' Myrtle sniffed. 'How could I do that to Ian? It would destroy his reputation. And Wally's.'

Yours too, thought Liz, but kept that to herself.

'Surely it's better to let sleeping dogs lie?' pleaded Myrtle.

'And let the killer go free?' Liz couldn't believe she would even suggest it. 'Think for a minute. The murderer killed your husband *after* he killed Ian. Why would he do that?'

Myrtle shrugged.

'There can only be one reason. He didn't get what he was after.'

Myrtle's eyes opened wide. 'You mean he never got the girdle?'

Liz nodded.

'I never thought of that.'

'Maybe Ian wasn't up there to put the girdle back in the museum. Maybe he didn't have it with him. Maybe the killer came looking for it in the antique shop, and Wally disturbed him.' Liz paused for dramatic effect, then brought out the big guns: 'What if he comes after *you* next?'

That obviously hadn't occurred to Myrtle. She looked horrified.

'You have to go to the police,' said Liz.

Myrtle was silent.

'It's the only sensible thing to do.'

Myrtle nodded slowly. 'I suppose you're right.'

'I *am* right.' Liz patted Myrtle's hand. 'It won't be easy, I know that. But surely it's not worth risking your life for?'

Myrtle sniffed and nodded. 'I'll go to the police station now.'

'Good,' said Liz. 'You know it's the right thing to do.' She thought about offering to go with her to the station, but decided against it. She'd rather not cross paths with DI Flint if she could avoid it.

'There's still one thing I don't understand.' Myrtle's brow furrowed. 'If the murderer doesn't have the girdle, who does?'

A very good question.

'I have no idea,' said Liz. 'But I'm not even sure it matters. The important thing, surely, is to stop the murderer from killing again.'

Myrtle's brow cleared. She nodded and dried her eyes.

21

After parting company with Myrtle, Liz decided not to head back to Kipper Cottage straightaway. There was something she needed to do first.

During their chat, Myrtle had told her she'd identified patients at the clinic with chronic or terminal illnesses and offered them treatment with the girdle. That worried Liz. Myrtle knew Benedict's wife, Katherine – Liz remembered her saying so at the White Horse and Griffin. Benedict and Katherine were both Christians. And Liz knew, from Tilly, that Katherine had suffered debilitating pain during her long illness. Had she been a patient at the clinic? Had Myrtle offered her 'treatment'? Had Katherine taken it? If that was the case, she needed to give Benedict a heads-up before the police followed through on anything Myrtle told them. The last thing she wanted was for him to be caught unawares and embarrassed by the whole thing coming out.

Even though it was only seven o'clock, the light in the town was already fading. Everything looked grey and washed out around the edges. Fog was definitely on its way – she could sense it coming, as much as see it. The sea was pewter grey and sullen, and everything sounded muffled. Even the seagulls were quieter than usual. Her knee was aching even more than it had earlier in the day, probably because of the increased humidity. She wished she didn't have to detour to Benedict's, but knew she had no choice. It was what friends were for. Even so, as she hobbled up the hill to Pannet Park, part of her was hoping Benedict wouldn't be in. She had no idea how she was going to tackle the subject of the girdle without sounding like a madwoman. Or, worse, an incurable busybody.

Her hopes were dashed when she saw lights on in the house. She limped up the path and rang the doorbell. How should she broach the subject of the girdle? Her mind had gone a complete blank. She sighed. And waited. No answer. She rang the doorbell again. Perhaps he wasn't in after all? She peered through the glazed section of the door, but could see no sign of movement inside. She rang again. Still no answer.

She turned round and headed back down the path with a sense of relief. She would try to call him when she got home. Or maybe she'd call Kevin and explain to him what had happened? He would know how to break the subject to Benedict. That was a great idea! Why hadn't she thought of it before?

'Liz!'

She stopped.

'Liz!'

She turned to see Benedict standing on his doorstep, naked except for a towel around his hips. Great.

She retraced her steps.

'Sorry I didn't hear you, ' he said. 'I was in the shower.' His hair was wet, and his bare feet were leaving footprints on the tiles. She tried not to stare.

'I'll come back later,' she said. 'I don't want to disturb you.'

'Don't be daft. Come in.' He waved her into the hall. 'Why not go and make us a cup of tea while I dry off. You know where everything is.' He headed for the stairs and was halfway up them when he called back, 'Or there's wine in the fridge if you prefer? Actually, I think I'd rather have a glass of wine. Be with you in a minute.'

Liz went into the kitchen. As usual, it was warm and filled with sleeping cats. She found a couple of glasses in a cupboard and went to the fridge. There were several things stuck on the door with magnets: tickets, receipts, a shopping list, and a snapshot of Katherine and Benedict together on a sailboat. They looked tanned and happy. Liz groaned. She opened the fridge and found a bottle of Chardonnay. She was looking for a corkscrew when she heard Benedict coming back downstairs. He was wearing jeans and a tee shirt. His feet were still bare, and his hair stuck up as he towelled it dry.

'Where have you been?' he said. 'I've left messages on your phone.'

'Have you? Sorry. I think there might be something wrong with it.'

He opened a drawer and gave her a corkscrew. 'I wanted to know what you thought of the support group on Saturday.'

'It was very ... supportive.'

He grinned. 'Not your cup of tea, then?'

'Not particularly.' She grimaced. 'Sorry.'

'That's okay. I suppose it isn't for everyone.' He dropped his wet towel onto one of the kitchen chairs. Liz resisted the urge to pick it up and drape it over the back so it would dry. 'It's definitely helped me, though. Gillian is great, isn't she?'

'Gillian?'

'The Reverend.'

'Oh. Yes.' Liz opened the wine. 'Very empathic.'

'Aren't you going to take your coat off?'

'Um ... yes. Okay. Good idea.'

Benedict gave her an odd look as he took the wine bottle from her. She gave herself a mental shake. She really had to pull herself together.

'I was quite surprised to see Myrtle Duguid there,' she said as she took her coat off. 'At the support group. Her husband's only been dead five minutes.' She realised how callous that sounded. 'What I mean is, I'm surprised she's even started to grieve properly yet.'

Benedict raised his eyebrows. 'I don't think Myrtle's the sort to let the grass grow under her feet.'

'I think you're right. You know her quite well, then?'

'Not especially. She was friends with Kathy.'

'Oh?' Liz tried to sound nonchalant.

'She had regular physio for her MS, over on the West Cliff. Myrtle's the receptionist there. I think they got to know each other pretty well.' He handed Liz a glass of Chardonnay. 'Cheers!'

She didn't really feel like drinking, but clinked glasses with him anyway, and took a sip.

'Is everything okay? You seem a bit ... on edge.'

'Do I?'

'A bit.'

Liz put her glass down. 'Actually, I do have something I want to ask you.'

He gave her a quizzical look.

'I think we'd better sit,' she said.

'That sounds ominous.'

She waited until they'd both taken a seat at the table, and took a deep breath. 'Katherine was a Christian, wasn't she?'

'Yeeees.' He was clearly wondering where this was going. 'We both are.' He corrected himself. 'Were.'

'The thing is ... the girdle. St Ælfflaed's girdle. It's

supposed to have healing powers. I've found out that Ian Crowby had taken it out of the museum, and that he and Myrtle were using it to scam people. Patients.'

Benedict had gone very still.

Liz ploughed on. 'Patients like Katherine, who came to the physiotherapist. They were charging them for "treatment" with the girdle.'

Benedict still said nothing. There was an intensity about him she'd never seen before. She wasn't sure she liked it.

'I've persuaded Myrtle to go to the police. She's there now. But I wanted to let you know what was happening, in case— ' she hesitated '—in case ...' She didn't know how to finish.

'In case Kathy was one of their dupes.'

'Exactly.'

Benedict nodded slowly. 'She was a good Christian. But she was also a practical woman. She didn't put her faith in miracles.'

Liz was relieved. 'I suppose she ...'

'She knew she was dying.' Benedict interrupted. 'She'd known it for a long time. There was only ever going to be one outcome, no matter how much faith she had, no matter how hard she prayed.' He slammed his fist onto the table without warning. 'Those *bastards!*'

He jumped up and started to pace.

'Bastards! Taking advantage of sick people like that. Of *dying* people.'

'I know.' Liz tried to think of something else to say, but it was hard to improve on those sentiments.

He continued to pace. 'I hope they lock her up.' He stopped. 'Actually, no. Prison's too good for her ... too good for people like her and Ian Crowby.' He practically spat the name. 'He got what he deserved. Exactly what he deserved. Divine retribution!' He laughed a little wildly. Liz stared, open-mouthed. She didn't know this man at all. He fell silent, rubbing his fingers. She realised he must have bruised them when he hit the table. She stared at his hands.

'You cut your finger, didn't you?'

'What?' Benedict looked at his hand. 'What?'

'You cut your finger. The night Ian Crowby was murdered. Chopping tomatoes, you said.'

He frowned. 'What are you ...?' His eyes opened wide. 'Oh, my God.' He dropped back into his chair and stared at her. 'The blood by the font. Surely you don't think ...?' He shook his head in disbelief. 'How can you think ...?' He rubbed a hand over his face.

Liz wanted to burst into tears, but held herself together. Benedict tried to take her hand. She moved it away.

His expression hardened. 'Okay. Look at me. Look at me, Liz. You said I have a tell, so look at it now. Look at my mouth *now*. Please believe me when I say *I did not kill Ian Crowby*.'

The left-hand corner of his mouth didn't twitch at all.

'*I didn't kill Ian Crowby, and I didn't kill Wally Duguid*.'

Still no twitch. He was telling the truth. Relief flooded through her and left her shaking.

'Okay?'

'Okay.'

He nodded. 'Katherine didn't take the girdle cure. She would have mentioned it if she had. We had no secrets from each other. We trusted each other.'

Liz flinched.

There was an awkward silence. He stood up. 'Okay. Thank you. For trying to warn me. It was well meant, and I appreciate it.' He picked up the wine glasses and took them to the sink. Tipped the wine out.

'Benedict, I'm sorry ...'

He held up his hand. 'I understand.' He was looking at her as if she was a stranger. 'I really do. It's fine.'

She knew he didn't understand. She knew it wasn't fine at

all. Nothing would ever be fine again. She just wanted to get out of there.

'I really am very sorry.'

She fled.

ALTHOUGH SHE'D BARELY BEEN in Benedict's house half an hour, the fog was much thicker when she came out. She stumbled up the path, hardly able to see more than ten yards in front of her. Haloes of moisture glowed around the street lamps, providing little in the way of illumination as she walked slowly back to the old town. She cursed herself for a fool. Of course Benedict had nothing to do with the murders! How could she even think it? She had to admit, though, that his anger had shaken her, particularly when he'd raved about divine retribution. It had brought back terrible images of Wally Duguid, dead eyes staring, and his mouth crammed with copper coins. Even though she knew, in her heart, that Benedict wasn't the killing kind, she hadn't realised just how little she really knew him, for all the hours they'd spent playing mah-jong and talking in the café. She sighed. That was hardly likely to change now. She'd be astonished if he ever spoke to her again.

She lingered for a while on the swing bridge, watching the black water slide underneath, listening to the slap of waves on metal. The melancholy, repetitive sound seemed to match her mood. She sighed. Everything had probably worked out for the best. She had no business looking for love again at her age. She and Mark had shared a once-in-a-life-time relationship – it was selfish and unreasonable to ask for more. She shivered. The fog had crept through her clothes and was clinging to her hair and eyelashes. 'Way to go, girl!' she scolded herself. 'Why not catch pneumonia, on top of everything else?'

She headed home and, five minutes later, put her key in the lock at Kipper Cottage.

'Nelson! I'm back.'

She expected to hear his usual yip of greeting, but was met with silence. Puzzled, she closed the door behind her and took off her coat. Perhaps Niall was taking him for a walk? But then she remembered Niall was working a late shift until eleven. Nelson couldn't be with him. So where was he? She cocked her head and listened. There was an unusual noise – a faint rasping sound – coming from somewhere. She followed the sound and realised it was coming from the cupboard under the stairs. She crept towards it. The door was closed. But the noise – whatever it was – was definitely coming from inside. It couldn't be Nelson. He would be making much more noise if he'd been accidentally locked in there. She held her breath and opened the door.

Nelson lay on his side, chest rising and falling, with that horrible rasping noise. The fur around his neck was stained red. With blood?

Too late, Liz heard the step behind her. She turned, and lights exploded behind her eyes.

22

Liz clung desperately to consciousness. It wasn't easy. There were more fireworks bursting in her head than in Edinburgh at Hogmanay. Eventually they cleared, and she managed to push herself onto her elbows.

'Stay where you are.' A figure loomed overhead, fuzzy around the edges. Liz blinked, and Myrtle solidified, smirking down at her. She had the sailing ship poker in her hand – was that what she'd hit her with? Liz put a hand to her head. It came away sticky.

'What ...?' She couldn't finish the sentence. She couldn't seem to string two words together.

'You thought you were so clever,' sneered Myrtle. 'Working it out. Naughty Myrtle. Naughty Ian. Conning those poor, sick people out of their money. But you only got it half right, didn't you?'

'You ... you killed them?' stuttered Liz. That didn't make sense, even to her battered brain.

Myrtle looked affronted. 'I did *not*. You were right, though – the killer didn't get what he wanted. I have the girdle. And there's nothing you can do to stop me selling it.'

'Myrtle ... no.'

'Aw, poor baby.' Myrtle's face twisted in mock sympathy. 'You're in no position to call the shots. People have told me what to do all my life. What to wear. What to say. What to think. But no more. In fifteen minutes' time, I'll have enough money to do whatever I want.' Myrtle's eyes gleamed with triumph. 'Whatever I want!'

She saw Liz's shocked expression. 'The buyer's waiting for me. You won't believe how much he's offered me for that tatty bit of cloth. And I don't want to be late. So sorry, Linda. I didn't want to do this, but you forced my hand, didn't you? Did you really think I'd go to the police?' She laughed and raised her arm to bring the poker down again. Liz braced herself for the blow.

A white blur streaked past her left ear.

'Nelson!'

The dog clamped his teeth onto the poker and clung on as Myrtle did her best to shake him off. Liz tried to push herself to her feet, but had to sit down again as the room spun sickeningly around her. All she could do was watch, horrified, as the life-and-death struggle took place in front of her. Nelson hung on to the poker. No matter how hard Myrtle shook it, he wouldn't let go. Even when she swung it against the wall, he clung on and rode it out. She did that once. Twice. And still, he wouldn't let go. In the end Myrtle was the one forced to release it. She leapt straight to one of the chapel chairs and grabbed it, brandishing it like a lion tamer. Her hair had come loose in the struggle and swung wildly around her scarlet face. Nelson spat the poker out. He advanced slowly on Myrtle, snarling, a bristling bundle of teeth and bloody fur. Liz hardly recognised him.

'Keep him off!' Myrtle screamed. 'Keep that animal away from me.' She jabbed the chair at him and backed towards the door.

'Nelson, come here.' Liz tried a coaxing tone. She didn't want Myrtle to hurt him any more than she already had. 'Come here, sweetie. It's okay.'

At the sound of her voice, Nelson swung his head to look at her. That was all Myrtle needed. She threw the chair in their direction and bolted for the door. Nelson was literally a fraction of a second behind her when she slammed it shut. The whole door shook as he bounced off it. Liz sobbed and ran to him, picking her way through the bits of her shattered chair.

'Good boy! Brave boy!' She hugged him tight. 'What a brave boy!'

He licked her face. She ran her hands over him to check for damage. She couldn't find anything apart from a bump behind his right ear and a shallow cut that had bled all over his neck. It seemed like a miracle, but maybe it wasn't – bull terriers were notoriously hard-headed. He looked extremely pleased with himself. He wriggled out of her grasp, scratched at the door, and growled.

'Oh, Nelson!' She hugged him to her again. 'Do you want a treat? You deserve a treat, don't you?'

He wagged his tail. She tottered to the kitchen cupboard and took out one of his dried pig's ears. She let him sniff it to see what it was, then tossed it across the room and bolted for the door.

She only just made it.

Out on the street, Liz ignored the barks of outrage coming from inside the cottage. Nelson would probably never forgive her for tricking him like that, but she really couldn't risk his being hurt more. The street swayed around her, and, thinking she was going to either faint or vomit, she bent over and took some deep breaths. Everything settled after a dozen or so lungfuls. Which was good. She had no time to waste: If she was right, Myrtle was in very serious danger.

She'd almost reached the bottom of the abbey steps when she saw a figure heading towards her through the fog. She froze. Was it Myrtle, back to finish her off? But no. The figure was too tall. Too tall and too athletic.

'Benedict!' Her voice was shaky.

'What the hell?' He hurried to join her. 'My God, you're bleeding! What happened?'

'Myrtle Duguid.'

'What?'

'She has the girdle. She's going to sell it. To the murderer!'

He stared at her.

'He's going to kill her, Benedict!'

'Where?'

She had no idea.

Benedict frowned. 'I saw someone go up the abbey steps just before I saw you. It was a woman, I think.'

'Come on.' Liz lurched as her knee buckled.

'Careful.' He took her elbow. 'I don't think you should be running around.'

'I'd like to see you stop me.'

He saw she meant it. 'Okay, but let's take it steady. She's only a minute or two ahead of us.'

They started to climb the steps as fast as Liz's knee allowed.

'Were you on your way to see me?' asked Liz. 'Just now?'

He nodded. 'I didn't like the way we parted at my house.'

'Me neither.'

They gave each other a rueful smile. Then Liz groaned. 'This is no good. We're not going to make it. You have to go without me. Go, and save her!'

'You're sure you'll be okay?'

'I won't be the one facing a murderer. Go!'

He leapt ahead, up the stone stairs.

'Your phone!' she shouted after him. 'Give me your phone!' Her own was in her coat in the cottage. 'I'll call Kevin.'

Benedict retraced his steps to give it to her, then bounded off again. Fog swallowed him almost straight away, but his voice floated back down to her. 'One nine zero two!' She realised it was the code for his mobile.

'Be careful!' she shouted.

Then she was alone.

The fog closed in, wrapping her in its numbing embrace. She kept climbing as she dialled Kevin's number. When he answered, she tried to keep her message as succinct as possible: Myrtle had the girdle; she was in danger; he had to bring police officers – lots of them – up to the abbey straight away!

'Where exactly?' he asked.

She wasn't sure. The museum? The car park? Then it came to her. 'The church. St Mary's! He's killed there before ... he knows the territory. For heaven's sake, Kevin, come as fast as you can!'

'Please, please don't do anything stupid!'

She hung up, not wanting to make promises she couldn't keep. She kept climbing, hearing nothing but her own heart pounding in her ears and her breath rasping. She forced herself to move faster, but it still felt like hours before she reached level ground at the top of the steps and saw Caedmon's Cross looming out at her from the fog. She stopped at the fork in the path. She couldn't see a thing, not even the gate to the car park, even though she knew it was right in front of her. She'd told Kevin to come to St Mary's. Was she sure about that? Something buzzed. It was Benedict's phone, still in her hand. A text from an unknown number.

I'M HERE, AS AGREED. WHERE ARE YOU?

She blinked. Read it again.
Everything seemed to slow down and stop.

23

Was Benedict the killer after all? Was the text from Myrtle waiting for him at their rendezvous?

If Katherine had received treatment with the girdle, he certainly had a motive. He believed in divine retribution. And he'd also cut his finger on the night the killer had broken the window in the church. Had he really been on his way to see her when she'd met him at the bottom of the abbey steps? Or was he going to meet Myrtle?

She tried to think clearly. Where exactly had he been when she'd seen him? Before the steps or after? She couldn't remember. But, surely, if he was the killer, he wouldn't have given her his phone? And his security code? There was no way he'd have wanted her to call the police – he would have killed her right there on the spot, wouldn't he?

And what about his tell? Earlier that evening, when he'd sworn he had nothing to do with the murders, the corner of his mouth hadn't twitched at all. She'd been sure he was telling the truth.

But what if she was wrong? What if he was killing Myrtle right now?

All of this flashed through her brain in a split second as she hurried along the left-hand path to the church. As she got closer, the ancient walls appeared through the fog. The lights were on, glimmering through the arched windows. The door was standing open. Liz took a deep breath and went inside.

Benedict was standing in the centre of the nave, staring at something she couldn't see, something at the front of the church. Hearing her footsteps, he spotted her and signalled urgently for her to join him. She hesitated, but only for a second. In her heart of hearts, she trusted him. If she was about to pay the price for that, then so be it. She hurried to his side.

Now she could see what he was looking at. At the front of the nave, near the altar steps, Myrtle was unconscious, but upright, held by a pair of strong arms. The strong arms of Ryan Goddard.

'Don't come any closer,' he said. He sounded very calm.

'Ryan ...' Liz began, and then stopped. She didn't know what to say. Benedict flashed her a helpless look. There was at least twenty yards between them and the couple locked in their strange embrace. Even if they rushed Ryan, he could kill Myrtle before they reached him. And then what? He was a big man. Much bigger, and younger, than Benedict. Even though there were two of them, it was still an uneven match. And Ryan would know that.

Liz took a step towards him.

'Ryan,' she said gently, 'do you really need to do this?'

'Someone does.'

Liz nodded. 'Maybe. But not you. Did your mum take the girdle cure?'

He hesitated before answering, clearly surprised that she knew. 'More than once.' His arms tightened around Myrtle.

'They took her money, and they gave her hope. It was cruel. And blasphemous. They deserve to die.'

'Isn't that up to God to decide?'

Unnoticed by Ryan, she'd taken another step towards him. Benedict glanced at her. That was a dangerous strategy. Liz ignored him, keeping her eyes on the other man.

'God?' Ryan gave a harsh laugh. 'How is he supposed to do that? A bolt of lightning? He *did* decide, and chose me as his instrument.'

'Are you the buyer?' Liz knew she had to keep him talking. 'The buyer Wally Duguid found for the girdle?'

'There is no buyer. I used their greed to undo them. Money is the root of all evil.'

A misquote, but Liz didn't think it was a good time to point it out.

'All people are greedy.'

'Some more than others. This silly—' he gave Myrtle a shake '—knew I was probably the killer, and she still decided it was worth the risk.'

Liz inched forward, with Benedict behind her.

'I knew your mum ... Jessy ... she was a good woman. What do you think she would say about all this?'

Liz was close enough now that she could see Ryan blink back tears.

'That's not the point. I'm doing it for her.'

'I understand, Ryan. I really, really do.' She nodded towards Benedict. 'We both do. We know what it's like to lose someone you love. To have to watch them die, inch by inch, every day.' She nodded at Benedict again. A prompt.

'You feel so helpless,' he said. 'It's a terrible feeling.'

'But it's natural,' chipped in Liz. 'A part of life. Not like this.' She nodded at Myrtle. 'Not like murder. Dying at someone else's hands is completely different. It isn't right, Ryan.'

'You say you understand, but you don't. Neither of you do.' He shifted Myrtle to get a better grip. 'When Mum died, it caught her by surprise. Even though she'd been ill for so long, she'd convinced herself it wasn't going to happen ... because of that bloody girdle. I had to see ... to see the look on her face ... when she finally realised it hadn't worked.'

He closed his eyes against the memory. Liz and Benedict crept forward again, like children in a twisted game of Grandma's Footsteps.

'I'm sorry,' said Liz.

His eyes flashed open. 'I know what you're doing. And it won't work.' His expression hardened. 'I know I won't get away with it now, but it doesn't matter. I can still finish what I started.'

He grabbed Myrtle around the throat.

They rushed him.

Benedict cannoned into him with his shoulder, Liz with her arms outstretched. Everyone went down. Hard. The impact jarred Liz, bringing her teeth together with a savage CLICK. She shook her head to clear it, and saw that Benedict had taken advantage of Ryan's momentary stupefaction to pull Myrtle's inert body away from him. Ryan scrambled to his feet. Liz tried to get out of his way, but not fast enough. Before she knew it, he had his hands round her throat and had dragged her to her feet.

It had all happened so fast, nobody could have stopped it.

She stared into Ryan's eyes so close to her own, so dark with desperation and rage.

'Ryan, no!' Benedict's voice came from a long way away.

The fireworks were back, exploding behind her eyelids. Ryan had his hands around her throat. He wasn't applying fatal pressure. Yet. But he could snap her neck in a heartbeat. She tried to keep the fear out of her eyes as they stared at each other. They stared and stared. As they did, she saw the anger ebb slowly out of him, turning the murderous man into a bewildered boy. He gave her one last, despairing look, then pushed her away.

She dropped to her knees and heard his running footsteps as he fled from the church.

'Are you okay?' Benedict hurried to kneel beside her. 'Dear God, Liz, I thought you were gone!'

'So did I,' she croaked. The look in Benedict's eyes – a contradictory mix of accusation and tenderness – was very, very gratifying. She forced herself back to the matter at hand. 'Get after him!' she gasped. 'He might do something stupid.'

Benedict nodded and ran out of the church.

Liz crawled to Myrtle, who was lying on her side. Blood was trickling from a gash on her forehead. It hadn't been there before, so Liz supposed she must have hit it when they'd tackled Ryan. She felt for a pulse in Myrtle's neck and found it. Where the hell was Kevin? Liz pushed herself to her feet and groped for Benedict's phone in her pocket. The screen was smashed. She must have fallen on it. Well, she would just have to take it on faith that Kevin was on his way with the cavalry.

She felt in her mouth and winced when her finger came out bloody. One of her back teeth was broken: she could feel it sharp on her tongue. Her head was thumping, every bone in her body ached, and she didn't even want to think about her knee. She looked down at Myrtle and prodded her with her toe. Myrtle didn't move. In Liz's professional opinion as an ex-nurse, she wasn't going anywhere.

Liz hobbled out after Benedict and Ryan.

OUTSIDE, the fog had almost cleared from the clifftop. Only a few tendrils drifted over the rough grass and clung to the gravestones. Liz stopped. She had no idea which way the men had gone, and there didn't seem to be any sign of Kevin or his reinforcements.

She cocked her head and listened. Nothing. Then ... faintly ...

'Ryan!' Benedict's voice. Coming from the clifftop to her right. Liz hurried towards it, past the place she had found Ian Crowby's body just a few weeks before. When she turned the corner of the church wall, she saw two figures silhouetted on the edge of the cliff, about forty feet away. Benedict was standing on her side of the wire fence, and Ryan on the other, dangerously close to the drop.

'This isn't going to solve anything,' shouted Benedict. 'Don't be bloody stupid.'

Liz didn't think that was going to help. She moved closer.

'Ryan,' she called as calmly as she could, 'come back over the fence. Please. Let's talk about this.'

'There's nothing to talk about.'

'That's not true. There's a lot to talk about. Like, how we can get you out of this mess. How we can make the police understand what happened. When we tell them about the girdle, they'll see ... they'll understand.' It was nonsense, of course, but Liz would have said anything to get Ryan back on their side of the fence.

He wasn't listening. He was staring into the still-foggy void below, his big fists clenching and unclenching. The sea was down there somewhere. A long way down.

'Please, Ryan.'

She saw his decision a split second before he jumped. Benedict must have seen it too, because he lunged towards him over the fence, managing to grab the back of his jacket just as he leapt. He jerked him backwards. They fell awkwardly, tangled in the wire.

'Hang on!' Liz ran to join them. She'd almost reached Benedict when she heard a noise. An odd rumbling sound.

'Get back!' Benedict's face twisted in panic. 'The cliff!'

The ground under her feet was moving. Sliding. She made one last desperate lunge for Benedict's arm, then threw all of her weight backwards.

She fell hard. Debris flew into the air, a choking cloud of dust and soil. Liz closed her eyes and tried to cling on to Benedict, coughing and gasping, but it was no good. Despairing, she felt his arm slip from her grip. The noise and vibration went on for ages – an eternity, it seemed. When it stopped, she opened her eyes. The dust and dirt gradually cleared. Benedict was still there, his eyes shut, clinging to the single remaining fence post. But Ryan had gone, swept down by the crumbling cliff into the sea.

'ALL THE RAIN we'd had, followed by the sudden hot weather, made it unstable,' said Kevin. 'It was only a matter of time before some of it broke away. That's what the fire brigade lads reckon, anyway.'

'Is Ryan ...?' Liz couldn't bring herself to finish her question.

'There's a team down there now, looking, but ...' Kevin shook his head.

She and Benedict were sitting on the tailgate of an ambulance in the car park, wrapped in blankets. Another ambulance had already left to go to the hospital, with Myrtle inside. She'd regained consciousness and was raving about her rights. Kevin had had to send two officers in the ambulance with her.

'There you go, Mrs McLuckie,' said Constable Williams, handing her a plastic cup. 'You too, Mr Ossett.'

Liz nodded her thanks, then turned to Kevin. 'What took you so long?'

Kevin and Williams exchanged a look.

Liz sighed. 'Flint.'

'As you know, she's not your biggest fan,' said Kevin. 'She said she wasn't going to send everyone off on a wild goose chase on your say-so. Eventually, I persuaded her just to let me and Bill come. Of course, by the time we got here ...' He tailed off.

'I wish we'd got here sooner,' said Williams.

So did Liz. Ryan might have killed Ian Crowby and Wally Duguid and also tried to throttle Myrtle, but not without reason. Nothing could excuse murder, of course, but he didn't deserve to die. And if Kevin and Williams had arrived earlier, he might not have done. Liz kept her thoughts to herself and sipped her coffee. She winced as hot liquid met broken tooth.

'You both need to go to the hospital,' said Kevin. 'Get checked over.'

'I'm fine,' said Benedict. He certainly looked okay to Liz: dirty but clear-eyed, with apparently not a bruise on him.

'I'm fine, too,' she said.

Everyone stared at her.

'Okay,' she capitulated. She knew she was a mess. 'But it'll have to be later. I need to check on Nelson first. Myrtle hit him with a poker.'

'Oh no!' Williams was horrified. 'Poor thing! I'll take you down there.'

'Just a bloody minute!'

They all froze.

DI Flint stood ten feet away, hands on hips, glaring at Kevin. 'I thought I said just the two of you on scene. It's like a bloody circus up here. No one's going anywhere until someone tells me what in God's name is going on!'

24

TWO MONTHS LATER

'This is the life!' Kevin leaned back and tipped his face to the sun.

'Don't get used to it,' said Tilly, 'just because it's your birthday.'

Kevin grinned and put his hands behind his head. 'I'll try not to.'

'Shall I unwrap this or leave it for a bit?' Liz asked Mags, holding up a lemon curd tart sealed in cling film.

'Better leave it for now, or the wasps will get it,' said Mags. 'Let's eat the sandwiches first. Can you stick it over there?'

Liz put it on the other side of the table. The table looked very pretty, laid with a green cloth and decorated with flowers and bunting. There was more bunting in the trees, which announced 30 TODAY! The garden was glorious, the lawn immaculate and flowerbeds bursting with colour. Birds sang. Bees buzzed. Liz sighed.

'You okay?' asked Tilly.

'Of course.' She dropped her voice to a whisper. 'Where's the cake?'

'In the fridge. B put it in there as soon as we got here.'

Tilly looked over to Benedict, who was helping Gillian Garraway set up glasses on a table on the other side of the patio. 'Do you think they're doing it?'

'Eh?'

'B and the Rev. Are they doing *it*?'

Liz gave Tilly a reproving look. 'How should I know? He does look happy, though.'

He did. He was tanned and relaxed in a cotton shirt and chinos, leaning in to hear something the Reverend was saying to him. She looked happy, too, and very different to how she usually looked, dressed in a strappy floral frock rather than her clerical collar. Liz had to admit she was attractive. Soon after the drama on the clifftop, it had dawned on Liz that the text Benedict had received was probably from Gillian, although she didn't know why it had come up on his phone as an unknown number. She'd never mentioned to Benedict that she'd seen the text, and would never dream of telling him what it had – briefly – made her wonder. Their friendship was still a bit wobbly, but mending. Liz had decided that if she couldn't have anything more, she was happy with that. In some ways, it was a relief.

'Cooo-ee.' Tilly prodded her. 'You were miles away, there.'

'Sorry.'

'I was saying that I heard Ryan Goddard is out of hospital now.'

'Really? That's great news.' Miraculously, the search-and-rescue team had found him alive at the bottom of the cliff, buried in several feet of soil and debris that had cushioned his fall. He'd been a mess, of course, but the hospital had managed to piece him back together. Now he was properly on the mend, he'd be standing trial for the murder of Ian Crowby and Wally Duguid and the attempted murder of Myrtle.

Myrtle had been charged for her attack on Liz, and her

trial was due to start some time in the autumn. Liz wasn't looking forward to testifying, but knew it had to be done. By rights, Myrtle should also be standing trial for fraud, but Gillian Garraway had persuaded DI Flint to drop those charges, arguing that her grieving parishioners had been through enough. Miraculously, Flint had agreed, although it was probably due more to pragmatism than compassion. She already had Myrtle bang to rights.

The girdle had been returned to the museum. Thanks to a donation from Janet Baxter – Liz assumed from her father's estate – its fragile condition had been stabilised, and it was about to be put on display for the first time in decades.

'Here you go, you two.' Benedict, followed by Gillian, came to give Tilly and Liz a glass of sparkling wine. 'Bottoms up.'

'Hey! What about me?' Kevin complained from his deckchair. 'I'm the birthday boy!'

'Hold your horses. I'm just getting you one. You too, Mags.' Benedict wandered over to the table. 'This all looks delicious. Is that mushroom and ham?'

Gillian smiled and raised her glass to Liz and Tilly. 'Cheers.'

'Cheers.' Liz took a sip of the chill liquid, trying to keep it off her newly crowned molar. Her dentist had only finished the work the day before, and it was still settling.

'Tilly,' called Mags from the table, 'what's in this pie again? I can't remember.'

'Ham, truffle and cheese.' Tilly hurried to join Mags and Benedict, to give them a detailed inventory of the rest of the feast.

Liz and Gillian smiled at each other, awkward.

'How's your knee?' asked Gillian.

'It's fine, thanks. Good as new.' Liz gave a wry smile. 'I didn't need St Ælfflaed's girdle after all.'

Gillian grinned.

Liz looked at her speculatively. 'I've been meaning to ask you about that.'

'Mmm?' The Reverend took a sip of her wine.

'Did you know about the girdle? About what Myrtle and Crowby were doing?'

Gillian pulled a face. 'I wish I could say I did. Two of my older parishioners told me they were seeing a special "therapist" and asked me if I believed in the powers of Christian relics. But when I heard the girdle was missing, I didn't put two and two together. I'm clearly not as bright as my mother likes to think I am.'

They laughed.

'What's so funny?' Kevin had levered himself out of his deckchair and wandered over to join them. His nose and cheekbones were red.

'Nothing much,' said Liz. 'I think you've caught the sun already. Don't you have sun cream on?'

'I forgot. Dad, do you have any sun cream?'

Benedict joined them to give Kevin a glass of wine. 'There's some in the kitchen. Do you want me to rub it in for you?' He grinned at Liz and Gillian. 'Thirty years old and I still have to watch him like a toddler.'

Kevin took a large swig of his wine and choked. Benedict slapped him on the back. 'See what I mean?'

When Kevin had recovered, he said, 'I'm starving. Isn't it cake time yet?'

'Cake?' said Liz, wide-eyed. 'What cake?'

Everyone laughed.

'Let's all go and have a seat in the sun,' said Benedict. 'Food always tastes better for a little anticipation, don't you think?'

While Kevin disappeared into the kitchen to look for sun cream, everyone else found a seat on the patio. They basked beside the many cats that were also dotted around, lying on the flagstones and various cushions. Tilly put her arm around Mag's shoulders with a happy sigh. 'Nice to have a day off. I wonder how Grazyna is getting on.' Grazyna was their new assistant manager, a capable and efficient – if rather humourless – woman from Poland.

'Don't think about that,' said Mags. 'Let's just try to relax, for once.' She turned to Benedict. 'What did you get Kevin for his birthday?'

'A new suit.'

'A birthday suit!' Tilly squealed, delighted.

Benedict grinned. 'He put a hole in the trousers of his old one, scrambling around on the clifftop.'

'A hazard of the job, I suppose,' said Liz.

'Like a certain detective inspector I could mention,' muttered Tilly. 'Do you know, the bloody woman is still sending me texts?'

'What kinds of texts?' asked Liz.

'Threatening ones. She's still trying to get me to admit we broke into Wally Duguid's shop. God knows how Kev works with her.'

'*For* her,' corrected Liz.

'Even worse!' said Tilly.

'Shh,' hissed Mags, then, more loudly, 'Here he is, the birthday boy!'

Kevin had emerged from the house and was rubbing sun cream into his face.

'*Please* can we have something to eat now,' he begged. 'I'm starving.'

They all made their way to the table and spent the next few minutes unwrapping food and setting it out on the serving plates. Kevin hardly waited until everything was out before he attacked it and filled his plate.

'This all looks fantastic. I am *so* ready for this.' He bit into a sausage roll and chewed. His eyes slid from Liz to Tilly and back again. Liz looked away, not wanting to catch his eye.

He swallowed and nodded. 'Lovely sausage rolls, Tills.'

Tilly looked at Liz, eyes wide. Had he discovered their secret?

'You'll have to give Liz the recipe,' added Kevin. 'I'm sure she'd like it.'

The three of them looked at each other; then Kevin's face cracked into a grin. 'You two! You can't lie for toffee. You really are terrible criminals.'

'I don't know,' said Liz. 'I have my moments.'

Kevin's eyes narrowed. 'I'm not sure I like the sound of that.'

After they'd eaten everything else, they brought out the cake and sang 'Happy Birthday'. Then they spent a very pleasant few hours sitting in the sun, laughing and chatting, before lapsing into more desultory conversation punctuated by companionable silence. Mags's head lolled on Tilly's shoulder, and she started to snore. Liz noticed that Benedict's hand had found Gillian's on the cushions of the swing seat. She tried very hard not to care, but failed. She waited a few minutes before she spoke.

'Well,' she said at last, smiling brightly and getting to her feet, 'this has been lovely. I could sit here all day, I really could, but I have to go.'

'Seriously?' said Kevin, disappointed.

' 'Fraid so. I have a delivery coming this afternoon. They couldn't give me a firm slot, so ... thanks for the food, Tilly. Delicious. Tell Mags I said so when she wakes up.'

'Will do.'

Benedict and Gillian both waved at her with their free hands.

Kevin nodded. 'I'll see you out.'

He walked with her, around the corner of the house to the side gate.

'Happy birthday.' She stood on tiptoe to kiss him on the cheek.

'Thank you,' he said. 'And ... sorry.' He held her gaze, his face serious. There was no mistaking what he was talking about. Liz thought about denying it or laughing it off, but decided not to.

'Don't worry,' she said. 'I'll get over it.'

She supposed she would.

Liz thought about it as she walked home. It wasn't as if she and Benedict had ever been an item, and in many ways he and Gillian were a better match. They were both Christians, for a start. And sporty. Something she would never be, even now she had both her knees working again.

Liz continued to walk, just enjoying the sights, sounds and smells of a seaside town – children laughing on the beach, seagulls, the tinkle of an ice-cream van somewhere on the West Cliff, the salty scent of the sea and sweeter aroma of candyfloss from the arcades. Whitby was at its very best when the sun was shining. She realised, probably for the first time, just how much the town had come to mean to her. In spite of its fog, rain, and gossip-mongering, it was exactly where she wanted to be.

She passed the entrance to White Horse Yard and noticed a For Sale sign there. Ian Crowby's cottage, newly spruced up by Iris, must have gone on the market. Liz hadn't seen Janet since her trip to Middlesbrough, which was something of a relief to Liz. She knew she'd hardly covered herself in glory at their last meeting.

Rather than continue straight down Church Street, Liz took a detour along Sandgate, past the Full Moon Café, where she could see Grazyna – a tall brunette – waiting on tables. In spite of Tilly's worries, it looked like she was managing very well. She was serving Iris Gladwell her usual scone – with jam, because it wasn't Friday. Liz grinned and waved at Iris and was about to turn away when a display in the bookstore part of the window caught her eye. It was an arrangement of charms and potions centred around something that looked like a small bundle of dried twigs. The label under it said '*Hand of Glory. A charm for the protection of thieves.*'

Liz's jaw dropped. There was no way Tilly would have paid seven hundred pounds for it, so ...? Had she stolen it the night they broke into Chapel Antiques? Or had she gone back to get it later? Either way, it was no wonder DI Flint was still on her case. Flint was a lot of things, but she wasn't a fool.

Liz went on her way, shaking her head. Tilly really was incorrigible. She promised herself she wouldn't encourage her in future, for Mags's sake.

Church Street was as busy as she'd ever seen it. August was the height of the tourist season, with school holidays and Trades Fortnight combining to create peak demand for sun, sand and sea. The bustle of crowds thinned at the bottom of the abbey steps, but not completely. There were still a few people coming and going along Henrietta Street, visiting the smokehouse, and coming in and out of their holiday cottages. The familiar aroma of smoking fish tickled Liz's nose as she put her key in Kipper Cottage's door.

Yip, yip, yip!

Liz thought she would never tire of that noise after the awful silence that had met her the night Myrtle had been waiting. She pushed her way inside, fighting her way around the leaping dog, who was wagging his stumpy tail for all he was worth.

'Down, Nelson! Stay still for a minute, for heaven's sake. I have something for you.' She took it out of her pocket – one of Tilly's telltale sausage rolls, wrapped in a napkin – and gave it to him. He wolfed it down.

She hung her bag and cardigan on one of the hooks and spotted something lying on the doormat. She bent to pick it up. It was a postcard from Athens, showing four different views of the Acropolis, addressed to '*Mrs Mac, Kipper Cottage, Whitby*'. A miracle it had reached her. She read it:

Weather grand. Work hard and dusty (never thought I would miss that Yorkshire mud!) Missing Nelson too. See you at Halloween. N x

Thanks to the fawning reference Dora Spackle had given him, Niall had secured a place on a dig at the Gymnasium of Lykeion. Liz's remaining ginger beer bottle had paid for his airfare. He hadn't wanted to take the money at first, until Liz capitulated and said he could consider it a loan. When he'd asked Liz how she'd persuaded Dora to give him the reference, she'd fudged and muttered something about Dora owing her a favour. She might tell him the truth one day, but if she was honest, she wasn't that proud of it. Who knew she'd be so good at blackmail?

She put the postcard on the mantelpiece over the inglenook fireplace. The fireplace looked just as good as she'd hoped it would, with its smart woodburning stove and basket of logs beside it, waiting for the weather to turn cold (which it would soon enough – this was Yorkshire!). The sailing ship poker hung on the wall beside the basket, a reminder to Liz of the perils of being too trusting: If she'd shopped Myrtle to the police as soon as she'd confessed about the girdle, she'd never have been bashed over the head with it. She'd promised herself she'd remember that whenever she used the poker. In fact, she wasn't likely to forget – Nelson howled like a banshee whenever she picked it up. Not surprisingly, the poker had joined Dora Spackle on his list of things he loved to hate.

Liz filled the kettle and put it on her brand new Aga-style stove. Then she took off her shoes and settled with a sigh on the single remaining chapel chair. She looked around her renovated kitchen with satisfaction. One room down, another nine to go – four in Kipper, and five in Gull. Liz was looking forward to it, and to the next chapter of her life in Whitby.

Who knew what adventures lay ahead?

AUTHOR'S NOTE

Whitby is, of course, a real place – a gorgeous jewel of a town nestled on the North Yorkshire coast, on the edge of the North York Moors National Park. It's most famous for being the birthplace of colonial explorer Captain Cook, and the inspiration for Bram Stoker's gothic masterpiece 'Dracula'. For those of you lucky enough to be familiar with the town, I've done my best to keep its geography – its street names and layout – as close to the real thing as possible. I may, however, have made a few mistakes and taken a couple of liberties, for which I hope you'll forgive me.

The White Horse and Griffin Hotel and the Duke of York pub are both real, immensely popular with locals and tourists. The Captain Cook Memorial Museum, Pannet Park, and the art deco paddling pool on the West Cliff are well-known attractions, and, of course, the abbey, St Mary's Church and the Abbey House Visitor Centre and Museum on the East Cliff draw visitors from all over the world. I have tried to describe them as accurately as possible. I feel I should mention, however, that the Abbey House Museum's real-life security measures are much more stringent than my fictional ones. I've also tweaked a few details about St Mary's Church – its font isn't big enough to drown somebody in, and its current excellent Anglican rector is a he, not a she. While we're in the mood for confessions, I also have to admit I have never been to Whitby Fish Market. As much as I love fresh fish, I love my bed more.

Kipper Cottage and Gull Cottage are based on the two cottages closest to Fortune's Smokehouse, on Henrietta Street. The Full Moon Café and the Copper Kettle café are my own inventions.

St Ælfflaed's girdle did exist. Several historical records tell how it was sent as a gift to Whitby's beloved abbess by her friend St Cuthbert. When she put it on, it healed her ailments. Unfortunately, like so many magical things, it has been lost to history and the mists of time.

I hope you've enjoyed spending time in Whitby with Liz McLuckie, and that you'll join her for her next adventure in the Kipper Cottage Mystery series – *Death at Neptune Yard*.

Until then, happy armchair sleuthing!

If you'd care to leave a review on Amazon they are enormously helpful in getting books discovered by new readers and I would be grateful for you thoughts.

ABOUT THE AUTHOR

Jan lives just outside Edinburgh with her husband, three kids, a one-eye whippet and a fat black pug. Born in a colliery village in the North East of England, she cut her literary teeth on the great storytellers of the 60's and 70's - Wilbur Smith, Frank Yerby, Mary Renault, and Sergeanne Golon. She began her writing career as an advertising copywriter, and has since had novels published by Random House and HarperCollins, and original audio series produced by Audible UK. She also writes for tv.

Jan enjoys psychological thrillers and crime fiction of all kinds, from the coziest of cozies to the blackest of noirs.

You can find Jan at www.kippercottagemysteries.co.uk

ALSO BY JAN DURHAM

Kipper Cottage Mysteries

Death at the Abbey (Book 1)

Death at Neptune Yard (Book 2)